SANTA PIG,
THE TRIALS OF
PATRICK WHITE

A TALE OF A VERY PERCEPTIVE PIG

Santa Pig,
The Trials of
Patrick White

A Tale Of A Very Perceptive Pig

Written and illustrated by

Suzanne Stephenson

Also by the author

Bearswood End

Mr Perkin's Takes Charge
A Cat's Judgement: Mr Perkins lays down the law

The World According to Patrick White
Santa Pig, The Trials of Patrick White

Forever Waste a comic legal novel

The Tale of Philida Thrush

Preface

The consensus of many religions is that God created both man and all the animals. Nonetheless, there is a division in religious books between clean and unclean animals. It seems that by and large animals are regarded unclean, not because of their habits but because of the type of feet they possess. It could be argued that whatever their feet, pigs have habits which some find unsavoury anyway, such as rolling around in muddy wallows and rooting around in the dirt.

However, some humans are disgusting in their habits. If a pig could talk, maybe he or she would not think much of the human race and would tell us all about it. Who is to say there are not talking pigs out there?

Chapter 1

How a pig can have such an involved life will surprise many people. One day someone might also find my diaries. Will they be interested in Emmie Martyns? Probably not. More likely they will be interested in Patrick, the pig. I sometimes mention this to my husband Alain. We are both lawyers, but you will know that if you have read anything I scribbled down in the past, or indeed if you are one of our friends or neighbours. If you have not read about Patrick before do not worry.

Let me explain. You will probably not believe what I am about to tell you. We live at Babblesprunge Farm in the village of Cobblemarkham. This is also the home of Patrick White the pig. I only work part-time as a lawyer because I run a small holding with pigs on it. One day Patrick White the pig started talking. You might have come across Patrick White on social media or the local news. He is becoming quite a famous pig, but he really does not like the notoriety. However, I know of no other pig who can talk. He somehow learned to talk after being left in a barn with the radio turned on; today I believe he prefers the television or to surf the internet.

I hope you will not be one of Alain's clients. Alain was recently made a KC with a London barristers' Chambers, and we all had a champagne celebration, except of course Patrick. On the other hand, I run a small solicitors' practice from home, concentrating on rural issues. Some of my clients would not mind about Patrick; some know already. I suppose a handful would not approve of their lawyer having a talking pig. For people who have not come across him before, I truly have a fully vocal, conversational pig and he has a lot of opinions. It was a shock to discover this.

My children are young adults. Alain says that he is not sure he likes my second business, running a small holding with pigs as it was keeping pigs which resulted in me having Patrick White at our farm. Aaron our youngest is just finishing the second year of his Sports' Science Degree. Letitia our second child is coming up to 21 and will soon finish her degree before studying for her professional exams. She will then join me in my practice. She already does some part-time legal work for me when she is not at university. Mathilda our eldest is 23 and will soon finish her pupillage in Alain's Chambers in London and be a fully-fledged barrister and it seems likely she will get a tenancy there.

If Alain had his doubts about my other business, this was reinforced by Patrick's trials and tribulations. If you know us or listen to the local news or look at social media you will think you know all about Patrick White, the talking dancing pig. But you won't know the half of it.

Patrick has had an eventful few months. Aside from finding his voice and his love of both soul and classical music, he has shown his ability at reading and indeed even took a star turn as an expert witness on porcine behaviour. The issue of piggy behaviour was important to the court case. The Court Hearing took place before His Honour Judge Winston Armstrong KC, a very tolerant and fair-minded senior judge.

I am not sure whether his husband and children knew of his piggy encounter. He seemed to have a rapport with Patrick. I will always remember the scene in the court car park with Patrick in his trailer and everyone involved in the trial assembled there. It was a shock for most people when Patrick started speaking, but His Honour took it all in his stride. Now His Honour has written to me.

If you have not met Patrick before is any of this making any sense? Probably not but keep reading.

Patrick found his experiences that day rather unnerving. He told me when we got home that he never wanted to leave the farm again and that he would devote his time to writing his memoirs something he could do with the voice recognition software on the computer Aaron's friend Charlie bought him. I suspect that he is now beginning to get his confidence back. My mother Rebecca who likes to pop in and bring Patrick fruit and veg from her garden reckons he is up to something, but she can't work out what he is doing seeing as he is confined to a brick barn, albeit in some comfort with a bath to wallow in, a television (also bought by Charlie), and computer equipment with voice controls.

Aaron agrees that Patrick is cheering up. He came home for the early May Bank Holiday weekend with his friend Charlie. The Honourable Charles Catton is a pleasant, wealthy young man who Aaron has befriended. While Aaron is sailing through university, the same cannot be said for Charlie who keeps having to repeat years. From time-to-time Charlie has a failed romance with some young girl who is probably after his money, but it is not just this that means he seems to be a permanent student. His generous spirit meant Patrick has more electronic equipment than some teenagers. To be frank Patrick is often quicker on the uptake than Charlie. Aaron will probably sail on to a career (quite literally) while Charlie will still study at university. Indeed, Aaron's first love is sailing. He tells me that he hopes to get into the world of business of charter yachts eventually.

I have been mulling over a number of things. Jim Birkshaw, a pig farmer from our village was trying to persuade me to take in a couple of young breeding sows from a friend of his. They are apparently pedigree Berkshires. Whereas I just dabble in pig farming, Jim has a big pig farm. I think I will ask Scuffy Dentson who helps at my little farm, and probably his dad, Flemmy as well. Animal rights activists broke into Jim's pig farm a while ago and there was a court case. It was in this case that Patrick gave evidence. Patrick is a Large White who I bought from Jim. Yes, what I said earlier is right and a pig gave evidence in a court case. More accurately rather than follow strict procedure the Judge spoke to him in the car park. After that incident Patrick has been cautious about leaving the farm. The journey to and from the court car park was strenuous for him.

Jim Birkshaw tends to stick to Large Whites, but it seems he has a friend who has a pedigree herd of Berkshires, but now his friend is retiring. Berkshire pigs are an old breed, rather smaller than Large White pigs. They have a mainly black colour often with white socks or the odd white patch and upright rather than floppy ears. Berkshire pigs are an old breed of pig which were favoured by Queen Victoria, but fell out of favour after World War II, but now people are bringing back the old breeds.

I don't know whether to have the Berkshire sows or not. I probably will do so, but I have some niggling doubts that something is not right.

I have also mulled over the letter from His Honour Judge Armstrong KC. It says,

'Dear Mrs Martyns,

Forgive me for writing to you out of the blue. You will no doubt be relieved it has nothing to do with any case or your appearances in court; at least not directly. I should also explain from the outset I am not writing in a judicial capacity at all.

You may not be aware that I also hold an Academic seat at Wastemooreland University as Honorary Professor of Law, and that I lecture there from time to time. I also run twice yearly moots or mock trials which tend to take place on Saturdays. These are quite a job to keep fresh and interesting. It is also the case that many of the students are an apathetic lot who will have a job dealing with the challenges of the real world. There is something to be said for people who have had to achieve success through what used to be called "the University of hard knocks." I am not sure the students would attend my events at all if it were not for the drinks and eats laid on after the moots and mock trials.

I was extremely impressed with Patrick the pig, and although I am not sure of the wisdom of having a pig as an expert witness. It was even a surprise to me how well he spoke and how intelligible his speech is. I was also impressed with your handling of the situation. I have no idea how some of these spoiled young people would cope when faced with a talking pig. So, I was thinking if it would be possible to enlist the help of Patrick and yourself to liven up a mock trial? I was hoping we could aim for September or October to stir things up for the Freshers?

We have a large lecture theatre at Wastemooreland University which I use for mock trials. It is not as far away from your address as my court. The back door of the lecture theatre opens straight out onto a car park at the edge of a playing field so the environment would be better for Patrick. There is plenty of greenery around.

I was hoping you might persuade Patrick to play the defendant, and I was hoping to enlist you to perhaps play a part, perhaps a witness for the defence. A couple of students would play Counsel for the prosecution, and of course the defence, but I was not going to tell any of them in advance the nature of the defendant. I would be the Judge of course, and the student audience would be the jury.

What would be the crime? I was considering assault occasioning grievous bodily harm. Patrick would be accused of biting someone who manhandled him…something along those lines. The papers might suggest he was caught stealing apples from an orchard, but then bit someone when they tried to push him out of the way.

Would you and Patrick the pig be up for this? I know it is a lot to ask. I emphasize I shall entirely understand if your answer is in the negative. I know you will also have to consult Patrick. You never know he might even find it a bit of fun. I would certainly provide him with some fruit from my garden too.

Yours sincerely,

Winston Armstrong KC'

I was having these niggling feelings that one gets that something is not quite right. I ascribed it to something to do with the Berkshires' and the letter, yet somehow, I felt there was something else. I could not shake it off. I had been waking up when it was first daylight with the feeling that someone had been walking about outside the house, yet when I got up in the morning there seemed to be nothing wrong outside. Patrick was in the brick animal shed just behind my Victorian house. No-one had apparently tried to break into the house, the shed or the animal enclosures down the field. My dog Piecrust had not barked. On a couple of occasions when I had been disturbed by this feeling, I noticed Piecrust looking towards the window and wagging his tail as if there was someone familiar outside. The cats were no use. Empress, Duchess and Princess just led me to their bowls early in the morning.

I talked about my niggling feeling to Alain, before he left for

London where he was appearing in the High Court, but he just raised his eyebrows and said I must be imagining things. My mother Rebecca arrived. She was less dismissive but could not come up with any answers.

Rebecca, Scuffy and I sat down with mugs of coffee on a bench in the garden, just behind the brick sheds, and discussed the Berkshires.

"My dad said you should be cautious," said Scuffy.

"Yes, I know I should be careful," I replied, "but I want to keep on good terms with Jim."

"Should it not be the other way around?" queried Rebecca. "You did very well for him when he was being sued."

"True," I said, "but I don't have the advantage, you have of knowing people on the Parish Council and I want to generally keep on good terms with everyone in the village."

Rebecca raised her eyebrows. "You don't have to deal with the Chairman and the Clerk," she said of her experiences as Parish Councillor. "One of my friends is on a Town Council in North Lincolnshire, and her Clerk and Mayor sound great. Apparently, their Clerk was Clerk of the year, and their Mayor is a very sensible lady. Whereas here at Cobblemarkham we have Colonel Snyppe as Chairman and Benjamina de Hotote as Clerk. They are… how do I put it… characters."

Her friend's Town Council sounded much more professional, but less entertaining than our local Parish Council. I was aware Colonel Snyppe was well known in the village since he had also taught Maths at the grammar school in town after leaving the army and was now retired from teaching as well. Benjamina sometimes bought eggs from the farm-gate. She appeared to be what old books would describe as a spinster and could be seen cycling around the village as she did not own a car.

"Well," I continued, no longer focusing on the Parish Council, "I want to stay on good terms with Jim so I shall buy the Berkshires."

I decided to ring Jim as soon as I had a moment. I then mentioned my other concern.

I took a mouthful of coffee. "But what about this person wandering around the farm?"

"Now you come to mention it," said Scuffy, "I have found the door to Patrick's shed open twice. He did not seem too bothered and claimed he knew nothing about it. I just thought someone 'ad forgotten to shut things up, so I didn't mention it."

"Funny that he wasn't bothered," I said and looked at Scuffy and Rebecca. "Are you thinking what I'm thinking? Could it be Patrick?"

"There is a high possibility," said Rebecca. "He knows how to use his mouth for a lot of things other than just eating, so it is not impossible that he has found a way to undo bolts and latches."

Indeed, he could use an implement to tap on a keyboard and to write a signature.

I decided to mention His Honour Judge Winston Armstrong KC's request. Scuffy sucked his teeth and shook his head but said,

"I'll take him in a trailer if I really must."

Rebecca said,

"You should let Patrick make the decision. If he doesn't want to go, then that is the end of it. However, I do suspect he may be your early morning wanderer."

Rebecca and I discussed matters further and decided to see if we could catch the culprit. Nobody was to mention our suspicions to Patrick. When the time was right, I would discuss the judge's letter with him.

Rebecca came to my home that night with her red setter dog, Selwyn. We both bedded down in the big living-room downstairs after sharing a chicken pie and half a bottle of rose. I wished Alain and Aaron were at home in case we were wrong in our suspicions. We bedded down with clothes on and flashlights to the ready. I also made sure we had a poker and rolling pin nearby 'just in case'. Of course, our phones were to hand.

As I dozed in the darkness, I could hear our dogs gently snoring. At first, I heard a nightingale sing, and then it was quiet but then a barn owl kept hooting. It was a fine still night and I thought I could even hear bats flapping about. I slept fitfully until dawn and then I got up and sat close by the window in my office at the rear of the house looking and listening. Rebecca stirred after a while and stumbled in from the living room and came to sit with me.

There was the beginning of a glow of light outside which kept increasing through the mist and murk of dawn. The birds were chirruping. At first, I thought we would not catch anyone. But after I while I thought I heard a scraping and a creaking noise… as if a bolt was being slid back and a door was being opened. Then I heard a shuffling footstep. I was not sure, but I thought I heard a grunt.

"I think Patrick is out," hissed Rebecca. "What should we do?"

"Let's try and confront him outside," I said. "I want to catch him in the act."

We quietly came out of the house, using the front door which was out of sight of Patrick's quarters. We crept around the side and spotted Patrick's large piggy hind quarters ambling gently down the track to the fields where I kept my other animals. Many were in their shelters still asleep. Mabel the pony and Martha the donkey had stirred, and Martha came to the gate and rubbed noses with Patrick. Patrick sniffed the air when he stood outside the sows' paddock, but they did not stir. A rumble of snores came out of their pig ark, where Gina and Lola lay sleeping. I could see him nosing at their gate and I heard him grunting.

If he had wanted to do so, he could have forced his way into the paddock. I suspected that even electric fencing would be no impediment and that he was strong enough to push the gate inwards. However, he grunted and turned round and began a leisurely stroll back towards his quarters.

Rebecca and I stood in the middle of the track. Pigs tend to be short-sighted, so he did not seem to notice us, and a light breeze was blowing in the other direction carrying our scent away from him. As he got closer, I spoke to Patrick,

"Going somewhere? Were you?"

There was a loud grunt followed by the reply, "Can't an *oink oink,* fellow go on an early morning stroll?"

"Patrick, you had me worried, I thought there were intruders at the farm," I replied.

"Intruders?" said Patrick. "Don't you worry, Emmie if there ever were intruders, I would protect you… *oink.*"

"Why were you wandering the farm?" I asked as we strolled back to his quarters.

He replied, "I assumed I was not a prisoner… and sometimes I crave fresh air and the company of other animals."

I was not sure whether to believe him. I showed him back to his quarters and gave him the benefit of the doubt. I fed him some pig food and old potatoes and was relieved that at least there was no burglar. That was just the start of things.

Chapter 2

After finding Patrick had been out in the small hours I sat down and had a serious talk with him, about the perils of wondering about outside his quarters, and I also warned him that if he broke into any other animals' quarters, he could find himself under lock and key. Alain said I should have just fitted a padlock, but I was well aware Patrick could break one anyway. I just hoped good sense would prevail. I also discussed the letter from His Honour Judge Armstong KC. I thought Patrick would just turn down the request. Instead, he said,

"It requires careful thought. I have been getting a bit bored. I am also interested in the wider world, but I don't want to cause you trouble or have trouble myself."

He paused, "Could we not ask the Judge over so I could talk it over with him?"

I agreed (with some reluctance) that we would ask His Honour to come for tea one day. It was another complication I could do without.

As it turned out the acquisition of the Berkshire sows was not without its pitfalls. Jim Birkshaw arrived in his red pick-up truck on a pre-arranged date to await his friend Ted Grufferton. Ted arrived in a battered Land Rover pulling an animal trailer which was mostly caked in mud. He got out of his Land Rover, and I could see that he was wearing overalls as mud caked as his vehicle. He had a misshapen nose which was hard not to stare at, and very bushy white eyebrows. He cleared his throat,

"Hello, thank you for taking Doreen and Delores. I've got to be honest with you. Doreen is a decent breeder, but Delores has only been in pig once… and she had just one piglet which died. I'll only charge you for Doreen. They are kind of inseparable… so I'll throw in Delores."

I had suspected there was a catch. I was suspicious that Jim had known all the time. I did not want to become the owner of the home for odd or useless pigs, but for the sake of good terms with Jim, I said to Ted,

"Well, just this once… I don't normally take in pigs I can't use."

I could see Jim and Scuffy smirking slightly in the background. It was as if everyone else was in on a joke except me. Doreen and Delores were let into a paddock adjacent to Gina and Lola's paddock. I made sure the electric fencing was switched on, and that all the formalities of movement licences were complete. Although I offered Jim and Ted tea or coffee they left quite quickly.

As I passed Patrick's quarters a voice said,

"I can smell lady pig… *oink*."

"There are some new sows at the farm, Berkshires," I replied. "You are not to go bothering them, unless you have permission."

There was some grunting and then some music was turned on in Patrick's shed. I didn't know if there was any significance to Patrick's choice of music, Sam Cooke's 'A Change is Gonna Come'.

I always enjoyed seeing my son, so I was pleased when Aaron appeared for the weekend with Charlie Catton. Alain was home for a while as well and I was aware Letitia should be joining us too. Her exams were due to take place shortly so she would not be home for more than one night. Once her exams were over, she would move out of the university accommodation and come back to the farm. I would not say it to His Honour Judge Armstong KC, but I felt Letitia was at a rather better law school than the one at Wastemooreland University.

We did have a rather odd piece of post that week I raised with the boys and nearly gave Alain apoplexy. It was a card from the Returning Officer at the local market town which was the home of the district council. It confirmed adjustments to the electoral roll. In addition to Alain and myself being on the electoral roll it seemed Aaron, Letitia and a certain 'Patrick White' had been added. I understood if Letitia and Aaron wanted to vote in their home constituency, but I was concerned as to the appearance of Patrick's name.

As we sat down to dinner and Alain poured out some wine, I asked, "Anyone know how Patrick has got onto the electoral roll?"

Alain nearly dropped the bottle.

"I did ask Aaron to make sure my name got added to the form when a letter came here," said Letitia.

"What form?" said Alain angrily. Aaron looked very sheepish.

"Well," he said, "a few weeks ago I noticed a card on the hall table inviting the householder to log in and check the details on the electoral was up to date... It was when Charlie was here... and well, Charlie and I thought... I mean it was just a bit of a laugh... we added Patrick as well as Letitia and me..."

"Yes," said Charlie, "I think it's a huge laugh." He looked as goofy as ever.

Alain had his head in his hands. He said,

"It's not a laugh... I am trying to figure out if you boys have committed an election offence. I think the best we can do is just all keep quiet about it, after all I don't think that Patrick is going to vote."

Alain glowered at Aaron and Charlie. Later he said to me that he had seriously contemplated asking Charlie to leave our house, and never return, but he did not wish to cause a rift with Aaron, who regarded Charlie as his best friend. He indicated that he did not see how there could be further ramifications from their actions; little did we know what might follow later.

I told Rebecca about the boys' actions as I walked into Cobblemarkham Village Hall with her a few days later. She laughed at the story. I had decided to attend one of her Parish Council meetings. Someone had purchased the former Vicarage (long since replaced with a modern house in the centre of the village). It was a large Georgian edifice which had fallen into disrepair, but it had four acres of land which abutted the 'A' road leaving the village. Developers had acquired it and were applying for planning permission to convert the old building into four luxury flats and to build two executive houses in the grounds. The public were allowed to attend Parish Council meetings. I thought I ought to find out what was going on about the planning matter, since I had clients very close to the site, although in principle the proposal did not sound too bad to me.

The Village Hall was in fact the adapted Victorian schoolhouse, converted in the nineteen seventies to a much-needed hall when the primary school moved to more modern premises. The hall had an entrance hall with toilets on one side of the doorway and a tiny kitchen plus a door leading to a staircase on the other side. I had never been upstairs, but I understood there were two small offices upstairs, one used by the Parish clerk from time to time and the other by the hall trustees if needed. The main part of the building was the high-ceilinged hall which boasted a small stage on the far side which actually took up about a quarter of the space. The front door and the windows to the hall area were tall arched affairs with a point at the top, rather like those of some churches.

The Councillor's chairs and a table had been arranged on the stage and a small table and chair had been placed just below the stage. I believed from prior conversations with Rebecca seating arrangements had been at the behest of Colonel Snyppe. Benjamina de Hotote was already seated and was glowering up at the stage. Although it was a warm June evening, Benjamina pulled a lavender coloured jacket closely around her and did not take off her purple felt hat which had some ornament attached to its band which looked rather like a bunch of miniature carrots. As Benjamina had slightly buck teeth I found myself thinking of rabbits in mauve outfits.

Rebecca clambered up onto the stage and sat towards the end of the table. I sat with half a dozen members of the public on chairs in the body of the hall. Councillors continued to arrive and take their places. They were an assortment of different ages and types of people from a sporty looking young man still clad in his cycling shorts who had evidently cycled his way to the meeting to a frail looking elderly white-haired lady who needed a lot of help from Benjamina and Rebecca to get on the stage and to her seat. Colonel Snyppe was the last to arrive.

He was an elderly man with a small moustache dressed in a tweed outfit even though it was a rather warm night. Sporting a pair of small round spectacles, he took off a tweed hat to reveal an almost bald head with just a few straggly pieces of grey hair. He put down a bundle of papers done up with string on the table and removed the string with a flourish,

"My hair-ribbon, don't you know!" he said. The other Councillors gave polite laughs.

He looked at the clock which said about five to seven, and said, "Right, class, time for the National Anthem."

Benjamina fidgeted and said, "I have mentioned before that it's not in the rules." She did not say anything about his use of the word 'class'.

"Well, it's just outside the meeting time... so I say it's okay... so get up everyone."

There was a shuffling of seats, and everyone stood up except one of the people sat near me. He had a t-shirt emblazoned with the words 'Not my king'.

"God save our Gracious King..." began the colonel in a booming baritone voice. Everyone else except the one man mumbled along to his singing.

After the National Anthem had finished there was a scraping of chairs as people sat down again. The colonel looked up at the clock which made a slight 'ting' as its hands reached seven o'clock and then he banged a gavel.

"Right time to start," he said booming out again.

"Let's start with apologies, Madam Clerk..." There were no apologies for absence. He then sought declarations of interest from his fellow Councillors of which there were none either.

"Now we come to public participation..." But before the colonel finished his sentence, the man who had sat during the National Anthem jumped to his feet.

"My name is Simon Christianson, and I protest," said the man "I am a Republican and when I moved here from Birmingham I didn't expect this sort of thing," except he sounded as if he said, "My name is Sigh-mon Crease-tionson and 'oy protest."

The colonel made a spluttering sound and Benjamina said, "I have mentioned this before... the National Anthem is suitable for national occasions, and we do not have provision in standing orders for it to be sung at monthly Council meetings." She looked rather pained and was almost visibly sighing. A couple of other Councillors tried to speak but she waved her hand at them and went, "Shhh."

"Well," the colonel said not stopping to get the views of the other Councillors or to confer again with the Clerk, "we will save the National Anthem for occasions you don't attend Mr Crease-tionson, but is there any other public participation? The limit is fifteen minutes."

Simon Christianson mumbled something almost audible under his breath about prejudice against 'Brummies' and then got up and left the hall, slamming the door noisily.

A couple of other members of the public asked to speak about the planning application. They were concerned that the design of the new houses should be in keeping with the Georgian Vicarage. I agreed with their comments, so I did not find it necessary to speak myself. I was also aware that my mother was likely to express some sensible views.

The next thing to happen was approval of previous minutes of the Council. Then Colonel Snyppe read out a written report from the Ward Councillor on the District Council, which referred to trying to get potholes mended in the village, together with a weight limit on the eighteenth-century bridge over the old canal. He added looking at the public over the top of his spectacles,

"It seems, class, the poor fellow couldn't be here as he is at his mother's funeral today."

It sounded as if the Ward Councillor had a lot on his plate.

I wondered when someone would remind the colonel that he was not still teaching maths at the grammar school. However, we quickly moved on to the planning application and nothing was said to the colonel about how he addressed the meeting. I saw my mother Rebecca's hand shoot up. The colonel scowled at her but let her address the meeting. She spoke calmly and sensibly about the conversion of the Vicarage building itself to apartments being a better fate for the building than going to 'rack and ruin' but pointing out that the Council could still express concern over the design of the new buildings.

After the various Councillors had spoken the colonel banged his gavel on the table and said,

"Let's take a vote."

The Councillors voted to object to the application on the grounds the current design would harm heritage of the site but noted if the design matters were addressed support would be offered to the application. The remaining members of the public except myself then chose to leave the meeting. As a courtesy to my mother, I chose to remain until the end of the meeting.

It was about 9.30 in the evening by the time I reached home, and as I approached my house, I had a view down the track. It was apparent that the door of Patrick's shed was wide open.

"Oh, no," I said to Rebecca. I had asked my mother home for coffee. "It looks like Patrick has let himself out. I'm sorry but we better go and find him."

We walked down the track to the other animals' pens. At first, I could not see Patrick. I could see the other creatures and the Large White sows snoozing in the entrance to their pig ark in a pile of hay. As we got closer to the paddocks and pens, I could hear a fair amount of grunting. Doreen was standing in her pig ark grunting and squealing and looked agitated. Patrick was pressed up close to the gate as was Delores on the other side of it. They were nose to nose. There was some heavy breathing and a few grunts from each of them. They appeared to be gazing into each other's eyes.

"Patrick," I said. "What did I say about not letting yourself out...? And also, I told you that I don't want you bothering Doreen and Delores."

He turned his head and said, "I am not bothering Delores. We are just getting acquainted. I think it's just her mother who is protesting... *oink snort, snort.*"

"Well, you need to go back to your quarters. Now!" I said emphatically.

"Oh, botheration. I didn't think you would be outside this late," said Patrick. "Why are you ... *oink...* walking about with Rebecca so late?"

"I have been at the Parish Council with Rebecca who is a Councillor," I said.

"What is a Parish Council?" asked Patrick with a snort.

"If you go back to your quarters, I will tell you all about it," chipped in Rebecca.

"Oh, if I must," sighed Patrick who grunted and started to waddle back down the track. He looked sadly back at Delores who seemed to return his gaze and who made a little grunt which almost sounded wistful. She seemed to bow her head down and head back towards the pig ark.

As we reached the shed, he added, "I shall promise to be good if you chat with me a bit and tell me all about Parish Councils."

I was not sure I believed him, but despite the absurdity of the request a lawyer and a Parish Councillor found themselves sitting down with a pig and explaining how the lowest tier of local government worked.

Patrick sat with rapt attention and asked the odd question from time to time.

"I can see that having local people make decisions about their local place makes sense, but that Colonel Snyppe person sounds as if he is well overdue to be made into sausages from what you say, and it sounds like animals need some representation on the Council," he quipped and then added, "I will try to be good really I will. I just thought it was good manners to introduce myself to the new girls. I would like to see that Delores again, but I could hear I upset Doreen. I will do my best to be a good and sensible pig."

I think he saw the dubious expression on my face.

"I promise I will be really polite and helpful when you ask that judge to tea," he added.

I remembered I had not yet asked His Honour Judge Armstrong KC to tea. I made a mental note to do so as I bolted the door to the brick shed closed with Patrick hopefully shut up for the night.

Chapter 3

*A*m I getting too interested in humans?

Since I learned to talk, I had a number of adventures and initially thought that I would lead a quiet life and write my memoires. After a short time, I could not help renewing my curiosity about the human world. My life was otherwise going to be limited to time inside my barn. There is only so much watching television one can do and only so much surfing the internet. After all, there had to be enough material to go in my memoires.

I had learned how to use voice controls for much of the media devices, and I also could move a computer mouse with my snout. I could use a pencil with my mouth in a limited way and would sometimes use a trotter to play with a small ball with Aaron and Charlie when they visited. The door of my quarters was in two halves, stable door fashion. I started to consider how it opened and closed, and if I could work any mechanism myself.

The top half of the door was left open except in very bad weather and had a simple latch which could be operated from either side. The bottom half was the main issue. As well as a simple latch I had a large bolt on the outside, which was mostly drawn up tight, presumably to keep me inside. I considered the problem carefully. If I got up on my rear trotters and rested my front trotters on the door, I could bend my head over the top and pull the bolt open with my mouth. The door would then open with a gentle push. I had a practice at doing this when no-one was around. It was not difficult for me. Soon I made a few trips around the farm late in the evening and early in the morning. In due course I hoped to go for walks around the village.

In the meantime, it was lovely to have fresh air and re-acquaint myself with the paddocks and other animals. I particularly enjoyed my strolls once Delores arrived. There was something about her. It was not just that she was a sow, and I was a boar...but she seemed special. I went to rub noses with her, but I was caught! I resolved that I needed to learn how to close my door as well as open it, since I intended to continue my visits to Delores. It was not just her scent and appearance which attracted me, but I noticed that she was listening when I tried out some human words on her. For the time being I would keep my views to myself and not mention my view about Delores to Emmie. I knew Emmie had enough to do; she was arranging for the Judge to come to tea.

When the day came for the Judge to visit, Emmie brought two more folding chairs into the barn in addition to the picnic chair Rebecca liked to use when she visited. I understood Rebecca might join us, but Alain was away sailing for the weekend with Aaron. She put up a folding table and covered it with a red and white checked cloth. She set out two teacups and saucers presumably for the Judge and herself and placed a sugar basin and a tin which said "biscuits" on the front on the table. There was also a cake under a cloche.

"What do I get?" I asked, knowing this was for Emmie and the Judge. My mouth was watering because I could smell the food. I

*resisted the temptation to knock down the table and steal the biscuits
and cake.*

*"I have not finished," she said, and came back with various bowls.
One bowl contained carrots and a swede.*

*"You can have something from this bowl," she said. I grunted a
kind of half approval.*

*Another bowl was full of large strawberries and early plums. There
was also a bowl with a handful of wizened apples and few tomatoes.*

*"All the fruit and vegetables are from the garden... they have not
been indoors so humans or pig can eat them. I took suitable bowls
outside to collect them and here they are!" smiled Emmie.*

*"Ah... snort... good," I replied with approval and asked if there
might be any beer.*

Emmie looked a mite cross and shook her head.

*"No," she said emphatically. "We are entertaining a senior judge,
not a mate of Aaron and Charlie. By the way, don't try to help
yourself in advance."*

I snorted in response.

"Best behaviour," she added.

*Emmie also insisted on washing my face as I had seen human
mothers do to their children. I found it quite an indignity. I had
wallowed in my bath earlier. I could not see it made much difference if
I had bits of straw and hay stuck around my snout. However, I let her
squidge a sponge over soapy water over my handsome visage.*

"Mind my eyes," I grunted.

"Okay, okay," she answered and was soon finished.

*"Now I am off to change my clothes and make myself presentable,"
she added. She returned a short time later in what female humans call
a 'dress'. The human concept of clothes is very odd. When I get hot, I
sweat through my snout. I have fat and some bristles to keep me*

warm. I suppose on a very cold winter's day I could understand that a knitted jacket might be nice. But I really didn't get this obsession with different clothes for different occasions and this frequent changing into clean clothes. However, when Emmie came back smelling of flowers in her clean dress, I was polite and grunted,

"You look pretty." She smiled. Then I spoiled things by sneezing sending bits of hay and straw onto the tea table and into Emmie's hair. She grimaced and quickly swept away the bits and then pulled some out of her hair.

"Sorry, oink," I said. "It was that flowery smell coming from you."

She smiled. "I am sorry, Patrick, it is my perfume," she said.

I really can't understand why female humans dowse themselves in half a bottle of flower garden. I mean if Delores rolled in a flower bed it would not make her more attractive to me. I like her scent of lady pig. Emmie smiled at me, and I could hear the sound of a car drawing up at the farm.

"Ah," she said. "That must be His Honour."

She left for a few minutes and came back with a man in a grey suit. At first, I did not recognise the judge because he was without his wig and robes, but almost within an instant as he got closer, I recognised His Honour Judge Winston Armstrong KC. Hanging a few feet back was a young man with dark hair tied back and a little earing; he had a smart close-fitting suit on and looked slightly uncomfortable.

"Hello, Patrick, or should I say, Mr White?" said His Honour. "Remember me? I have Jake Daniels from the University with me acting as my Clerk today. He will take a few notes."

At that moment Rebecca appeared. Emmie made a few introductions and hastily fetched a further chair and cup and saucer. Rebecca didn't seem nervous meeting the Judge, but I suppose he did not look that impressive in normal clothes. Jake Daniels was much quieter than Charlie and Aaron. I thought I would try to 'break the ice' with him as humans say.

"How... oink... are you... Jake? Do you prefer turnips or swedes?" I asked him.

"I am not sure I like either," he stammered.

"Oh, Patrick!" said Rebecca. "Leave him alone... I am sure he is not used to talking to a pig."

"I was only trying to be friendly," I replied. I was a bit nonplussed when His Honour started laughing.

"Oh, Patrick," said the Judge. "I think I am going to have a whale of a time with the students at the mock trial."

All the humans sat at the tea table and had human-type refreshments. I had a carrot, then I had a swede. And then some apples and then tomatoes which I don't mind admitting I chomped at enthusiastically.

The Judge outlined the plan.

"If you are willing," he said, "Jake will help me make up some statements for a pretend crime. The crime will be a theft which consists of the defendant breaking into an apple orchard, but he will be caught in the act by the owner of the orchard who will try to stop him escaping. The defendant will resist being detained and will bite the orchard owner in the hand and the arm, causing him to have stitches in hospital..."

"Stitches?" I queried. "Isn't that sewing?"

"It is also for holding wounds together," said Rebecca.

"The biting will result in an additional charge of assault occasioning 'grievous bodily harm'. What we won't tell the students is that the defendant Mr Patrick White is none other than Patrick White the pig!" said the Judge. "It will do Jake's colleagues good to be shaken up a bit."

Jake nodded as if to agree but he looked doubtful.

"So," I asked, trying not to grunt too much. "Will there be a pretend policeman to take me and lock me up?"

"No," said the Judge. "The pretending won't go that far... although I am hoping Mrs Martyns will play along with this too."

I was a bit hesitant about things, but I knew this Judge person was important to Emmie.

"I would like to accommodate your ideas," said I trying to sound a clever pig for the benefit of the Judge. He started to laugh and so did Emmie and Rebecca. I did not know 'why'.

Emmie said, "Perhaps, Your Honour we might go inside now and make more detailed plans."

"If you don't mind," I said. "I would like Jake to stay a few minutes to get to know him better."

Emmie, Rebecca and the Judge headed to the house.

"I have student friends... oink... you know. Aaron and Charlie are a bit older than you. They are not frightened of me," I said. I told him the name of their university.

Jake replied, "It's just that I have never met a pig before... let alone a talking pig. I have lived in a town all my life. I live in a flat in a big block."

"Then it's a good thing you met me... I am a very civilised pig," I said, and I managed to get a smile out of Jake. I added, "If the big block is flat how do you get into it?" Jake explained something of flats and blocks of flats to me.

"Shall we have some music?" I said to lighten the mood.

"Eh yes," said Jake "What do you have?"

I replied, "Classical... or Soul... James Brown? Ben E. King? Diana Ross? The Supremes?"

"I love music from the past like the Supremes and the Kinks. I

collect vinyl," said Jake. I didn't know quite what he meant; it sounded rather odd to collect plastic. However, I got some music playing.

First, we played Supremes' tracks like 'Baby Love' and 'Stop in the name of love'. We eventually were playing Diana Ross' 'Chain Reaction' very loud, and we were both dancing about to it. We did not hear Emmie, Rebecca and the Judge reappear. The Judge looked quite surprised.

"Patrick, turn it off," yelled Emmie.

Jake looked most disappointed as I turned the music off and turned to the Judge. "Sorry, Your Honour," Jake said. "I have to admit I was having fun with Patrick the pig. I hope I have not done anything wrong."

His Honour smiled and said everything was fine. I hoped it was too. However, I had other things on my mind.

"No... not at all," said His Honour, "it's just perfect. We have hit on a plan. You are going to be Counsel in the mock trial, possibly defence but maybe not. Emmie will be my Clerk on that day and her mother has agreed to play the defence witness. The papers will be a bit of a collaboration although I am afraid, Jake, you might get most of the work."

After that there was some further discussion of arrangements before everyone left apart from Emmie of course. I was not sure I like the idea of being tried for theft and assault even in a mock trial, but I went along with things for the sake of Emmie in particular. I did so hope that my visit to this local university would not be as troublesome as my visit to the real court, but my mind soon turned to other things.

But to what was on my mind... the fact was I could not help thinking about Delores. It was not just her scent, but she seemed *altogether different from other pigs. I felt I wanted to get to know her better and I wondered if I could even communicate with her on a higher level than other pigs and tell her a little of my experiences with the human world. I was aware Emmie and Flemmie were not altogether happy to have her since she seemed to have little capability of producing piglets; I felt there was a risk she might be sent off to be made into sausages.*

I waited until it was quite late. Everyone on the farm was hopefully asleep except me. I quietly let myself out of my quarters and trotted up the farm track.

"Oink... Delores," I called quietly. She trotted out of the pig ark where Doreen seemed to be fast asleep.

"Would you like to come to my place for a bit?" I asked. She grunted in the affirmative.

I slid the bolt of the field gate back and she came trotting down the track with me.

First, I showed her round my quarters and then I offered some apples to eat. I put music on quietly and we both did a little dance. When the birds started the dawn chorus and then Emmie's cockerel Lucifer crowed, I escorted her back to the enclosure she shared with Doreen. I was careful to re-bolt the field gate.

Whenever I had the opportunity, I would fetch Delores to my quarters. Sometimes I would keep her some tasty fruit prompting queries as to whether I was getting greedy overnight since in the morning all my snacks would have disappeared. Sometimes we would listen to music or take turns to use my bath. Delores was fascinated by my television, so we often watched television together. I was quite the gentleman with her which would have surprised Scuffy and Flemmy. I was very interested in how she followed my lead when I attempted to sing along with human popular songs. Now and again, I had my turn with the sows up the field. As it happened, I was more interested in Delores as company. It was not just her scent of sow, her beautiful dark skin and her pricked-up ears which appealed, but also her wish to learn and take an interest in my world which was part way between the human world and the animal world.

For a long time, Emmie didn't have a clue what was going on. I was very careful to keep gates locked and for us not to be seen together. When Rebecca, Letitia, Aaron and Charlie visited I said nothing to them. I would not have said anything anyway to Mathilda as I knew she had her reservations about me. Emmie seemed very busy with her "cases" which seemed to largely consist of old farmers arguing about bits of land. Now and again Emmie and I would have a discussion about the mock trial and what we needed to do.

One night when Delores came to visit, I had a huge heap of carrots in my quarters. I think it was meant to be a reserve for the next month, but Scuffy hadn't put it away. Delores and I were both hungry for a snack, so we decided to set to work on the carrots. We both ate so much we lay down in exhaustion and fell asleep. Before I knew it, it was morning. I had forgotten to get Delores back to her quarters.

Emmie walked through the doorway into my abode. She obviously saw Delores because I could hear a, "What." She also saw there were hardly any carrots left because I heard her say, "Greedy pigs."

Delores stirred and stretched. A loud 'parp' noise emanated from her behind. She yawned and then she looked Emmie in the eye and said,

"Hello, honey."

Chapter 4

Part 1

The Shock of Another Talking Pig

I don't know what Alain is going to say but it seems we now have two talking pigs. First, there is a little matter of Patrick bringing Delores to the animal shed where he lives. He has taken no notice of my requests to him to behave. Then there is a potential issue of Delores producing piglets. The only good thing is I was told she did not breed well so that might not happen. I had been debating whether to see if she should be rehomed in a petting farm. I felt I had been naively used to re-home an animal who was a little old to be a bacon pig but was no good for breeding.

"Why is Delores here, Patrick?" I asked.

Patrick had a sort of guilty look. "Well. *Oink... oink.* She likes it with me, and I get lonely."

I continued, "How long has this been going on? Have you been teaching her to talk?"

Patrick grunted, "She has been visiting for a while... and she can talk a little... can't you, dear?" He turned to Delores.

"I speak *grunt...* hello, goodbye... Patrick, honey?" she said.

"Do you know my name?" I asked her.

"Emmie," said Delores looking me in the eye "I... *snort...* Delores."

I wondered how long it would be before Delores could speak as well as Patrick. I decided to have a council of 'war' and summoned Scuffy, Flemmy, my mother Rebecca and my daughter Letitia who was at home for a couple of days having concluded her exams, and before leaving for a holiday. There was less surprise to the discovery Delores could talk, than the original discovery that Patrick could talk.

"Hello, honey," said Delores to each of my council of war.

"What else can you say?" asked Scuffy.

Delores grunted and said, "Apples," with an oink.

"Anything else?" he probed.

"Oink *oink* Delores... like apples food. You friends?" she said.

"That's enough asking her questions," I said. "But, Patrick, you clearly taught Delores some speech... and brought her to your shed... what is your view about what happens next?"

"What happens next? What do you mean?" he asked. "I want Delores here."

Letitia said, "I think Mum is concerned that you don't teach all her pigs to talk and frankly there could be a huge amount of public interest... and trouble... if it was known we had a farm full of talking pigs."

I did not dare think about it. Patrick looked thoughtful and said, "While I don't think the rest of the other pigs are bright enough to speak, because I am a very clever pig, and Delores is quite special too. If Delores were to stay with me, there would be no need for me to visit the rest of the farm. I promise I would not go wandering about the farm anymore if she can stay."

"What do think?" I said to Scuffy and Flemmy. "What of the risk of piglets?"

Flemmy said, "I don't reckon that sow be good for awt 'cept keeping that talking bugger company."

Rebecca was laughing and said, "I think you are going to get your own way, Patrick." Which of course he did.

I was not sure how I would explain all this to Alain.

Part 2

I keep my word... well, sort of.

I gave my word to Emmie that I would not wander about the farm anymore if Delores stayed with me. I was pleased when Delores was allowed to stay and indeed, she settled in very well with me. She learned more words and enjoyed television and music. She was not as interested in learning to operate the computer. I don't think Delores will ever be an intellectual pig like me! However, she has an easy-going nature which the humans like.

I am not sure what Alain thought. He called in late one evening clutching a glass of Scotch and said to me,

"Got a girlfriend now! As long as you are not going to ask for driving lessons."

"I don't think so," I said. "The driving seat area in cars looks rather a squash... oink... for an ample gentleman like me... and it all seems rather dangerous." I couldn't help thinking of car chases on American cop shows.

Rebecca called in to see us a few days later and Delores showed her improved skills.

"Honey... oink... how you?" she asked in a slightly 'singsong' voice with a slight American accent.

"I'm fine. How are you?" replied Emmie's mother.

"I fine, sugar," said Delores.

Rebecca asked me, "Why does she call people 'honey' and 'sugar'?"

I answered with a grunt as best as I could. "I think she watched some American TV shows... there was a lady on a couple of them who Delores reckoned looked a bit like her... so I think she is imitating her."

I did not mention to Rebecca how Delores would attempt to sing along to certain songs on tv and radio and that it absolutely sounded terrible. Rebecca would find out soon enough.

Rebecca asked Delores, "Do you enjoy television?"

"Grunt... uh ha," replied Delores.

Rebecca produced some fruit from her bag and Delores and I soon made it disappear.

Emmie appeared briefly and asked her mum, "What do think of the plan by those two women to turn their house and garden into an animal rescue centre?"

I pricked up my ears.

"I am not sure the colonel will like it... still, we have yet to discuss it," said Rebecca.

Rebecca continued, "'The Granary Manor' had been semi derelict before Derry and Terry Mossesson acquired it... I think Derry is the mum and devotes her time to animal rescue and Terry is the daughter... they say she is a veterinary nurse, but I am not sure at which practice. I have never seen any young children, but I have seen a middle-aged man in what looks like an airline pilot's uniform. I think he is Derry's husband or partner... they look alright, and they seem to have started clearing a lot of old junk and undergrowth from the place."

"What is there for the colonel not to like?" asked Emmie.

"Well," said Rebecca, "he doesn't like animals... he says dogs make him sneeze. The garden of that place is as big as a small paddock. I think the Mossessons want to put some housing there for cats and dogs, but also for small farm animals."

"I think that is a good idea," said Emmie. "Townies do silly things like try to keep turkeys in their back gardens or a pig in an allotment or worse still a flat, but then they can't cope."

"I don't think the colonel will like it," said Rebecca.

I grunted, "So this fellow doesn't like the idea of animals being rescued?" I asked. Rebecca nodded so I continued, "What do these townies do which means animals need to be rescued?"

Emmie replied, "People who live in towns often don't have the time or space to look after farm animals properly. Mind you, country people can sadly neglect animals too. Animals can come to harm if people don't know what they are doing or neglect them. It seems these people want to use their property to help some animals who need it."

I thought I understood but began to consider if I shouldn't go and see the premises myself. I had been thinking about exploring the village since I had promised not to go visiting the other animals on the farm. I decided the best time to go would be very early in the morning just as dawn was breaking.

Next morning seemed perfect. I knew Alain had gone away the previous evening and Emmie was on her own, without the youngsters. Scuffy had said something about "being a bit late." I awoke when the cockerels crowed, and the birds were singing the dawn chorus in the hedge. I undid the bolt to my quarters as quietly as I could so as not to wake Delores. Then I bolted the door to stop her coming to find me, if she awoke before I returned. I trotted up the track past the house to the road.

The first I had to do was decide whether the village was on the left-trotter side or the right-trotter side. From recollection of being in the trailer I turned to the right and started walking along the road.

I passed a couple of paddocks with ponies in them and then a terrace of cottages. There were a few larger houses in a variety of styles. Next there was an old looking building with grounds around it which I understood to be the church. It had a sign outside which said, 'St Erasmus of Cobblemarkham' and then gave times for what was described as, 'Sunday morning service' and 'Sunday evensong' (whatever that was). There was reference to a 'Prayer Group' and a 'Sunday School for children'. I did not think that children would want to go to school on a Sunday.

The next building was a pleasant white building with a lot of wooden tables and chairs in its garden. It had a sign saying, 'The Cobble Arms Public House' in big letters, and in smaller letters, 'Free house'. It smelled pleasantly of beer as I trotted near it. I knew from Aaron and Charlie about pubs, and I felt it would have been nice to go into one. I was surprised by the sign saying, 'Free house'; I thought one had to pay for one's beer.

Just opposite was a building with a high mesh fence and a sign which read, 'St Erasmus Primary School, Headmistress Miss Evertrout'. So, this was where humans sent their piglets for most of their learning. A house with what human's called a shop sat next to it, with what looked like living accommodation upstairs. The building sported a sign, 'Manny Sharma's Superstore, open 8 until 8 daily'. It did not look very super to me, but what did I know!

A little further on, there was then a new housing development on one side of the road and a farm driveway opposite. From the description I had heard, I believed it might lead to Rebecca's house. Not far from this driveway was a slightly churchlike building with a sign saying, 'Village Hall'. The density of buildings began to decrease with a row of small cottages being the last concentration of buildings. I believed if I trotted a great deal further, I would get to Jim Birkshaw's farm but soon I was in front of a sign which said, 'Granary Manor'.

The property immediately struck me as being similar to Emmie's house but shabbier. It had a track up the side which I decided to explore. I could soon see there was a big paddock area with some sheds that needed mending or pulling down. There was lots of room for animals. I turned around and came back down the track past the house. I had been lucky until now there had not been anyone about, but a man came out of the house and started to wipe the dew from the windows of what must have been his car. I made a dash around the corner and took cover in a ditch under the front hedge.

I must have made a slight noise, or the man was aware of some movement since he said,

"Who's there?"

Without thinking I said, "Patrick White, who are you?" and then I immediately regretted it.

He replied, "Sven Mossesson, I live here. What are you doing out there?"

I answered, "I'm just a local... I live at one of the farms... just taking a morning stroll, goodbye..." I stifled a grunt and lay as still as I could in the ditch until he had driven away. I was sure he hadn't seen me.

After my narrow escape I hastened back to the farm. Delores was only just waking up and she grunted at me and cuddled up to me. I seemed to have got away with it, or so I thought. As I had managed my stroll around the village virtually undiscovered, I therefore resolved to do it again in a few days' time.

Once again, I left Delores asleep and trotted through the village. It was very early, so there was no-one around. I had nearly reached Granary Manor when a truck suddenly appeared and before I could jump into a ditch it stopped right in front of me. I froze but to my relief I found it was driven by Jim Birkshaw's senior pig hand Greg, with Jim seated beside him.

"What are you doing there, Patrick, aren't you going to get into trouble with Emmie?" said Jim.

"I was taking a stroll... grunt," I replied.

"Well, don't you think we should give you a lift back?" he asked.

"I suppose... grunt," I said grudgingly.

"Best he got back before half the village notices and there is some sort of panic... open the back... and put down the ramp, please," Jim said to Greg.

"You won't tell, Emmie, please," I said as I made for the back of the truck.

"No, not straight away," said Jim. "Since I'm in a hurry to fetch some medication for a sow in difficulties... but later... if I don't see her today... she'll have to know."

"Trotters crossed he forgets," I thought, but did not say it.

I was just having this conversation and walking up the ramp when a car drew up behind the truck. A man got out. I recognised him straight away from my previous foray to Granary Manor. Sven Mossesson was clad in a smart dark blue uniform which had gold braiding.

"I knew I was not mad," he said in voice which sounded different from the other men I had met so far, which I was later told was a Swedish accent. "I spoke with him last week, but I could not see a person... I later thought I caught a glance of a pig."

"Yup," said Jim. "It's Patrick White, the singing, dancing pig who has been on social media and the local news."

"He talks a lot better than on social media," said Sven. "My wife and daughter will be envious I met him... and my colleagues on the plane will love to hear my story!"

"Plane?" said Jim.

"I'm a pilot. I'm just on my way to the regional airport to do a run to Stockholm and back."

I grunted loudly and interrupted, "Ahhem... grunt. Please do me a favour. I don't mind so much if you tell your wife and daughter about me since I hear they like animals but don't tell your colleagues while you are driving your plane."

"I will be flying, not driving," he replied. "But why do you not want people to know?"

"I don't want scientists to come and take me away... and find out why I am such a clever pig... oink," I said.

"Well, you were not so clever this morning taking yourself out here for a walk."

I conceded I had been very foolish. Sven promised not to tell anyone other than his wife and daughter of his experience. He seemed sympathetic to my concerns. He was soon on his way.

Jim quickly got me back to the farm. He backed his truck into the driveway and Greg got the ramp down. I quickly walked down and let myself into my quarters. As Jim was on his way, Delores opened her eyes and said,

"Hello, honey... oink... you been out."

Five minutes later Emmie appeared.

"It's odd," she said. "I thought I could hear Jim."

I didn't say anything.

Rebecca called in to say 'hello' a couple of days later.

"Oink. Hello..." I said. "Please could you do me a favour?"

I explained about my expedition to Granary Manor and how I was interested in the idea of an animal rescue centre, but how my secret expedition had gone wrong.

"Please could you ask the two ladies there not to tell Emmie how they know about me?"

"I will try," said Rebecca. "But you are getting bold and bad and if you keep it up you will get into trouble."

It was a good thing Rebecca spoke to Derry and Terry Mossesson because their interest in me had been piqued by Sven and inevitably they asked to see me. They seemed pleasant enough, but I was wary and kept my speech to the same level as that of Delores, although she was so shy she hardly said anything at all. Emmie promised to give them advice on pigs and donkeys of which they had limited prior experience. They did ask one thing.

"If we get planning permission to open the rescue centre, we will want to do some fund raising. Could we ask Patrick to sing a song on a promotional video?" asked Derry.

"What do you think, Patrick?" queried Emmie. "I know we don't want too much media exposure."

"One... oink... one little song," I responded. I thought it would make everyone pleased if I agreed this, and anyway I do like singing.

Derry and Terry went away smiling, and I vowed I would take it easy for the next few days, but that was not to be. First, Aaron and Charlie visited briefly.

I told them of my interest in local affairs. Aaron mentioned something called 'Parish Council Elections', and briefly explained matters to me. I said,

"Why are there no animal representatives on the Parish Council? After all we are in the countryside."

"Good point," said Charlie, laughing. "I think you would make an *excellent Parish Councillor. You are probably more sensible than anyone in local or even national politics."*

"Tell you what," he said, after a minute or two. "I've got an idea."

He told me what it was. I was not sure it was such a good idea, but I didn't think it would work out, so to please the boys I went along with it.

Then, Jake Daniels had arranged to visit to go over one or two things for the trial. He did not drive a car, so he had to take a bus to the bus stop in front of the pub and then walk the short distance to the farm. Emmie had made sure he had a chair and table and went to fetch him a coffee and a sandwich. I started to ask him about his journey.

"What are buses like to go in... oink?" I asked.

"Well," said Jake, "they work a bit like cars but lots of people can travel on them."

"A bit like pig lorries?" I asked.

"Sometimes," said Jake laughing.

"Hello, sugar," piped up Delores. "I... grunt. Delores." Jake nearly dropped his sandwich.

Emmie was just passing and said, "This one can talk a bit too."

There was a wry smile on Jake's face. He reached into a bag and handed each of us an orange fruit.

"It's a tangerine," he said. "I probably shouldn't give it to you but enjoy it..." We did.

Jake then began explaining the trial procedure and the order of speeches. He said would email Emmie the statements as soon as he had finished drafting them, so I would know what to say and what everyone else would be saying. Then he said,

"You will be asked questions to trip you up."

"Wont that hurt?" I replied. Jake explained cross-examination to me.

Finally, he asked me, "How do you feel about this, Patrick?"

I replied, "Feeling good... oink."

Delores piped up, "Grunt... Nina Simone?"

The afternoon finished with us listening to some of Nina Simone's greatest songs and only stopped when Jake said, "I guess I better head for the bus-stop."

He walked down the driveway to the sound of 'Don't let me be misunderstood' coming out of my quarters and as he disappeared out of sight, I could just hear him call,

"Bye, that was a great afternoon."

Chapter 5

This Trial seems all too real.

Being the custodian of two talking pigs, running a small-holding and a legal practice not to mention balancing family life with work, can be quite stressful. Alain is a little disdainful of my piggy sideline but doesn't try to make me stop; I think he accepts I could never part with Patrick and Delores. He brought me a nice bottle of Chablis when he came home from his latest trial, and we sat enjoying a glass. He said,

"It's a good thing that sow Delores is not as interested in humans as Patrick."

"Yes," I replied. "It's a job keeping him out of mischief. I hope he will co-operate with the mock trial. He seemed to get on well enough with that young man Jake Daniels."

I explained that I had received an electronic trial bundle prepared by Jake and that I would have to go through the papers with Patrick. Alain said,

"Almost like preparing for a real trial," he paused. "Ah well maybe this Jake will be less trouble than Charlie. I can't say I trust him after he put that pig on the Electoral Roll. When Aaron and Charlie were here, they were definitely up to something. I don't know what it was, but I am sure it involves that pig."

"Oh, do stop calling him 'that pig'," I said. "His name is Patrick White."

Alain raised his eyebrows, and I went to look at the mock trial documents.

The first document to meet my gaze was in indictment. There were a few things the purist might criticise, but it looked like Jake had tried his best to do a professional job. After I read the indictment, I read a fair selection of the statements which had also been drawn up carefully.

It was plain there were alternative charges on the indictment. There was very little hint in the statements that Patrick was a pig. I understood the 'mock transcriptions of police interview would follow later'. I also thought that Jake had injected a little humour into the statements using some quite entertaining names and seemed to understand a bit about Patrick's nature. There were some inconsistencies of detail ripe for cross examination. I hoped the Judge would find this work by Jake acceptable since I felt Jake deserved praise for his work.

Alain read some of the documents and said wryly, "Is there much difference between real Patrick and imaginary Patrick?" Then he added, "In the real world I doubt if the police would ever have come out to the incident."

Here are the main documents.

INDICTMENT

IN THE CROWN COURT OF
WASTEMOORELAND UNIVERSITY
The King
v.
Patrick White
Patrick White charged as follows:

1. Statement of Offence

   Robbery contrary to section 8 the Theft Act 1968

   Particulars of Offence

   Patrick White did on the 5th day of September steal apples belonging to ABC Apples with dishonest intent to appropriate the apples and immediately before or at the time of doing so, and in order to do so, he used force on Mr ABC and or put or sought to put him in fear of being then and there subjected to force.

2. Statement of offence

   Theft contrary to section 1 of the Theft Act 1968

   Particulars of Offence

   Patrick White did on the 5th day of September dishonestly appropriate apples belonging to ABC apples with intent to permanently deprive ABC Apples of the said fruit.

3. Statement of Offence

   Grievous bodily harm contrary to section 20 Offences Against the Person Act 1861

   Particulars of Offence

   Patrick White did on 5th September unlawfully and maliciously wound and inflict any grievous bodily harm upon Mr ABC Apples, by biting him.

4. Statement of Offence

Assault occasioning actual bodily harm contrary to section 47 Offences Against the Person Act 1861

Particulars of Offence

Patrick White did on 5th September unlawfully assault Mr ABC Apples by biting him.

WITNESS STATEMENT

CJ Act 1967 s9, MC Act 1980, ss5A 3(a) and 5B, Criminal Procedure Rules 2005 Rule 27(1)

Statement of Alphonse Brook Claude Apples

Age if under 18 Over 18 Occupation Director

This statement (consisting of pages signed by me) is true to the best of my knowledge and belief, and I make it knowing that, if it is tendered in evidence, I shall be liable to prosecution if I have wilfully stated anything in it which I know to be false or do not believe to be true.

Signature ABC APPLES Date 12 September

1. I am the proprietor and owner of the Apples' Orchard a large commercial orchard. On 5 September I was inspecting my crop to see if it was ready for harvesting when a heard noises which were a mixture of munching and grunting. At first, I could not see anyone as the defendant who I now know was called Patrick White was concealed by the trees.

2. I picked up a tree branch in case I had to defend myself and confronted the defendant. I said, "Drop those apples." Initially the defendant seemed to take no notice and carried on munching. I therefore got closer to him.

3. The defendant appeared to hear me and stopped munching and said, "I am hungry," but he picked up another apple off the ground to which I said, "That's no excuse, you need to be locked up," and I stood in front of him to stop him leaving and tried to take the apple from him. He said between munches, "I wouldn't put my hand there if I were you," which I took to be a threat.

4. It was at this point I felt his teeth connect with my hand. I sustained a serious injury by biting. I screamed loudly to warn off the defendant and summons assistance. I believed he would have attacked me further to get apples if help had not arrived.

5. Employees from my depot came running and chased the defendant into the far corner of the orchard where there is a shed where I understand he was detained. I was taken to hospital by my apple depot manager. I had twelve stitches for the wound to my hand and fingers and I was fortunate not to require plastic surgery on my little finger. I also had an anti-tetanus injection. It took 6 months for my hand to recover although I am left with some slight scarring.

6. I can confirm that no one is allowed to have apples from my orchard, even wind fall apples without my consent.

Signature ABC Apples Signature witnessed by PC 99 PLOOD

WITNESS STATEMENT

CJ Act 1967 s9, MC Act 1980, ss5A 3(a) and 5B, Criminal Procedure Rules 2005 Rule 27(1)

Statement of Barley Mow

Age if under 18 Over 18 Occupation Depot Manager

This statement (consisting of pages signed by me) is true to the best of my knowledge and belief, and I make it knowing that, if it is tendered in evidence, I shall be liable to prosecution if I have wilfully stated anything in it which I know to be false or do not believe to be true.

Signature B Mow Date 22 September

1. I am employed by ABC Apples as depot manager, and I supervise the loading and dispatch of apples from the apple orchard adjacent to the depot.

2. On 5th September I was supervising the men's tea break when I heard a loud yell from the orchard. I immediately put down the kettle and quickly went to the place where I thought was the source of the yell. The men followed as soon as they had safely stowed the teacups. We did not even stop for a second biscuit.

3. I was very surprised to see the boss waving a tree branch with one hand and with blood dripping down the other hand. The defendant who I now know to be Patrick White was protesting that he had been hungry, and he had only picked up windfalls. There was also a strange woman standing there.

4. We chased the defendant away from Mr Apples using fallen branches. It took 8 of us to chase the defendant into a tool storage shed in the corner of the orchard. I closed the door on him to await the arrival of the police. The defendant was

pushing the door so hard I thought he would break it open, so I put an old concrete roller against the door.

5. I then checked that someone had called the police and the ambulance and administered first aid to Mr Apples.

Signature B Mow Signature witnessed by PC 99 PLOOD

WITNESS STATEMENT

CJ Act 1967 s9, MC Act 1980, ss5A 3(a) and 5B, Criminal Procedure Rules 2005 Rule 27(1)

Statement of Everest Plood

Age if under 18 Over 18 Occupation Police Constable

This statement (consisting of pages signed by me) is true to the best of my knowledge and belief, and I make it knowing that, if it is tendered in evidence, I shall be liable to prosecution if I have wilfully stated anything in it which I know to be false or do not believe to be true.

Signature E Plood Date 12 September

1. I am Police Constable 99 Everest Plood stationed at Wastemooreland Police Station. I am part of the neighbourhood policing team for the villages in the vicinity. Acting on information from a member of the public I proceeded at 14.00 hours on 5 September to the premises of ABC Apples. This is the first opportunity I have had to write a statement about the incident.

2. I arrived at the same time as the alleged victim Mr ABC Apples was being treated by paramedics for his injuries and shortly before he was taken to hospital. As a result of what he told me I went in the company of Mr Barley Mow and three other men in his employ Mr Harry Bailey, Mr Tom Cobbly and Mr Andy All to a shed in the corner of an orchard.

3. The alleged defendant had been shut in the said shed and there was a roller placed against the door. He was evidently trying to push his way out and I could hear a lot of grunting and huffing from inside the shed, so I said,

"If I open the door, are you going to behave nicely and come out quietly" and he replied, "I will be nice if no-one else tries to shove me in a shed just because I picked up some rotten old apples off the ground." I therefore gently opened the door.

4. The defendant who I know to be called Patrick White seemed to rush out making a snorting noise, but he seemed to stop when he saw my uniform. I then said to the defendant, "I am arresting you on suspicion of theft and assault. You do not have to say anything. But it may harm your defence if you do not mention when questioned something which you later rely on in court. Anything you do say may be given in evidence." He responded, "I have not done anything wrong, but I suppose I better come with you if you insist."

5. I then realised he would not fit into my police car due to his size. I therefore made arrangements for him to return to his home. Later special arrangements were made for him to be interviewed under caution.

Signature E Plood Signature witnessed by PS 101 BOOT

WITNESS STATEMENT

CJ Act 1967 s9, MC Act 1980, ss5A 3(a) and 5B, Criminal Procedure Rules 2005 Rule 27(1)

Statement of Dr Ignatius Special FRCS

Age if under 18 Over 18 Occupation Consultant in Emergency Medicine

This statement (consisting of pages signed by me) is true to the best of my knowledge and belief, and I make it knowing that, if it is tendered in evidence, I shall be liable to prosecution if I have wilfully stated anything in it which I know to be false or do not believe to be true.

Signature I Special Date 29 September

1. On 5 September I had just come on duty at the Wastemooreland Hospital Accident and Emergency department after a week's holiday on my yacht when ambulance men brought a Mr Alphonse Apples into the Department. Mr Apples had already been seen by my Junior colleague Dr Ann Other, but he had been loudly protesting he wished to be seen by the Consultant in charge.

2. I noted that he had suffered severe lacerations to his right hand which had been cleaned and that there had been a moderate to severe blood loss. Fortunately, although the wounds required stitching the lacerations had narrowly avoided any bony injuries. I arranged for Mr Apples to have his wound stitched and to receive an anti-tetanus injection and pain relief. I also prescribed pain relief medication. I discharged Mr Apples and arranged to see him in outpatients 14 days later when the seven stitches to his hand were taken out.

3. When I examined his hand in outpatients Mr Apples hand was progressing well so, I discharged him to the care of his General Practitioner. In my professional opinion the wound was caused by a large bite from a person or an animal with a very large mouth and would be likely to leave modest scarring after 6 months but no other sequalae.

Signature I Special Signature witnessed by PS 101 BOOT

WITNESS STATEMENT

Criminal Procedure Rules r16.2: Criminal Justice Act 1967 s9

Statement of Mrs Rebecca Witness Occupation Semi Retired

Age of Witness; Over 18

This statement (consisting of pages signed by me) is true to the best of my knowledge and belief, and I make it knowing that, if it is tendered in evidence, I shall be liable to prosecution if I have wilfully stated anything in it which I know to be false or do not believe to be true.

Signed: RW Dated 5 November

1. I am acquainted with the Defendant Patrick White, and I make this statement about what I know of the events of 5 September.

2. I am aware that Patrick White does not know his way around the neighbourhood. It came to my attention he had gone out early in the morning before breakfast and had not returned home several hours later. Since this is out of character for Patrick, I started to search for him.

3. I was passing the orchard of ABC Apples when I became aware of a disturbance. I went into the orchard to have a look. The gate was wide open so anybody could go inside. As well as apples growing on the trees, I could see many windfall apples on the ground.

4. I went to where I thought I could hear shouting. I could see Patrick standing apparently eating an apple and a man who I believe was Mr Apples poking him with a large stick. Patrick was saying, "Why are you doing that? It's just a windfall and I was hungry." Mr Apples said, "I'm going to get it back," and Patrick replied, "I wouldn't if I were you, you might hurt

yourself if you put a hand in my mouth." However, Mr Apples tried to force his hand in Patrick's mouth, but he immediately yelled and withdrew his hand which was now bleeding badly.

5. I ran forward and said, "Patrick, stand still, the man has hurt his hand. I want to see if I can help him." Mr Apples kept waving the stick with his other hand and did not seem anxious for any assistance. Instead, he yelled, "Thief, help," at the top of his voice. It was at least half a minute before he let me step forward and wrap my scarf around his wound to stop the bleeding. Eventually some men from the apple depot appeared.

6. The men picked up branches and were poking Patrick who was doing nothing except saying, "I only picked up a couple of windfalls." The men chased him with the branches into a shed in the corner of the orchard and locked him into it, despite my protestations. The police were then called, and I assisted in arrangements to get Patrick home.

Signed RW Dated 5 November

WITNESS STATEMENT

Criminal Procedure Rules r16.2: Criminal Justice Act 1967 s9

Statement of Mr Patrick White

Age of Witness; Over 18 months Occupation Sus Domesticus

This statement (consisting of pages signed by me) is true to the best of my knowledge and belief, and I make it knowing that, if it is tendered in evidence, I shall be liable to prosecution if I have wilfully stated anything in it which I know to be false or do not believe to be true.

Signed P White Date 28 September

1. I make this statement about the events of 5 September. I would make it clear the events are still very clear in my mind. I want to make it plain I deny the charges against me and believe I have been greatly wronged.

2. I shall start by saying I don't go out and about very much. I tend to stick to my own farm. However, I do like to go for a little walk early in the morning when it is quiet. On 5 September I went out on one such walk. It was rather misty. I suppose autumn was starting. I became a little disorientated in the mist and could not find my way back home.

3. I seemed to be walking round and round. I was hungry and I was sure I had missed breakfast. I passed the entrance to the orchard I now know belongs to Mr Apples and noticed the gate was open. I could see apple trees laden with fruit and noticed a few apples on the ground. I decided to enter the orchard to see if I could just pick up and eat some windfall fruit since I was very hungry. The further I got into the orchard the more I saw windfall fruit on the ground, quite a lot of it going rotten so I

started to pick some up and began eating. I did not take any apples off the trees.

4. Suddenly I was confronted by an angry sounding man waving a branch who said, "Drop those apples." I was still munching but I managed to reply, "They are only windfalls. Sorry, I was hungry." The man, who I now know to be Mr Apples began to poke me with the branch and said something like, "I want to get it back," and started lunging at my mouth. I said, "I wouldn't do that if I were you, you might get hurt." He then shoved his hand between my teeth but withdrew it quickly with a tremendous yell. It was about this time I noticed my friend Rebecca had arrived. She told me to stay where I was.

5. Mr Apples was yelling, "Thief, thief, help!" while Rebecca was trying to wrap up his hand and stop it bleeding. Then some other men came who I understand were employed by Mr Apples. I tried to explain that I had only picked up some windfalls and I did not mean any harm. Mr Apples was still shouting, and they picked up some branches and started hitting me with them and chasing me into a shed where they locked me inside. I heard Rebecca protesting. I also became aware there was something heavy against the door because I could not open the door to get out.

6. After a while I could hear a man outside the shed who said that he was a police officer and asked if I would come out quietly. I recall saying, "I will be nice if no-one else tries to shove me in a shed just because I picked up some rotten old apples off the ground." He opened the door, and I rushed out of the shed. He then arrested me and cautioned me. I recall I co-operated fully even though I felt outraged that I was the one being arrested. I believe that I was the victim rather than the perpetrator of a

crime. The only thing I did wrong was eat a few windfalls without prior permission and which might otherwise have been thrown away.

7. The police officer wanted to take me to the police station, but I was too big for his police car. He allowed Rebecca to make arrangements to take me home. I was interviewed under caution on a later date.

Signed: P White Dated: 28 September

Chapter 6

Part 1
Why do I get into trouble?

*E*mmie and Jake Daniels having been going over the 'mock trial 'documents with me. I think that Jake is a reasonably good judge of my character. The fictional me and the real me have much in common. I do like early morning walks and apples. I hope I don't get lost like the fictional Patrick but if I did, I could imagine looking for windfall apples. Fictional Patrick found the human world interesting but also challenging, or he would not have got into such trouble. I think fictional Patrick is very like me.

Rebecca has told me not to worry too much about the mock trial. I think she has been thinking more about the local elections rather than my concerns.

I understand it has been the time when people have had to choose their Town and Parish Councillors. Not so long ago when I expressed an interest in local affairs, Charlie and Aaron had (so I thought) jokingly suggested I stood for the Parish Council.

"You could represent the animals," said Aaron with a laugh.

"That would surprise people... oink," I responded, drinking some beer from a bucket. Charlie always provided some welcome liquid refreshment.

Charlie said to Aaron, "What a hoot if we could get him on the list of candidates for Parish Council."

They did not pursue things immediately but one day when Letitia was there as well as Aaron, Charlie said to me,

"Hey Patrick piggy put a pen in your mouth and sign these papers... you too Letitia..."

Well, I signed the papers to please him, and I think Letitia never thought he would do anything with them, so she signed the papers too. Whether Aaron had an opinion it was hard to tell. He seemed to enjoy having Charlie around but was often talking about 'yachting events' and 'regattas' which meant nothing to me. I am not sure Aaron really grasped that for a human Charlie was not very bright, and that trouble seemed to follow him about.

One day quite some time later, Rebecca came to my quarters somewhat flustered and a bit red in the face. Delores said to her with a grunt,

"Hi, honey," and I said, "Hello, oink... have you brought any fruit?"

Rebecca looked rather cross which was unusual. "No, I have not, I am not at all pleased with you, Patrick," she said. "Why are you down on the list of candidates for the Parish Council?"

"Oh, no," I said with a grunt. "I shouldn't have signed things for Charlie."

I did hope this was not going to upset Emmie and Alain too. Alain could get particularly angry and had already threatened to ban Charlie from the house which could mean, no more beer.

Rebecca said, "That young man is causing so much trouble... fortunately there won't be an election per se, because the number of candidates were the same as the number of seats. I hope Emmie and Alain won't be looking at the candidate list... because to avoid trouble all you need to do is not turn up to sign the papers at the first meeting. Just send in a message to say you don't want to be a Parish Councillor after all."

It seemed sound advice and I was minded to take her advice, although I didn't actually send a message. It was not that I couldn't do so because these days I had an email address, it was that something within me held me back. However, then I received a visit from Derry Mossesson. She seemed to have been visiting Emmie about legal matters but decided to visit me too. I think she liked the company of Delores and myself.

"I'm sure it's that Colonel Snyppe stirring things up," said Derry to Emmie as they came into the barn. "He doesn't live far from Granary Manor and he has a fear of small animals, although the point of the application is to build proper facilities for any animals we help, such as a few kennels and a small cattery and a couple of suitable buildings for a handful of pigs and goats or sheep."

"How do you know he has a fear of small animals?" said Emmie.

"Well, you know the colonel is a good age and that although I am new to the village, as a child I lived in the town and went to the Grammar school where he was my maths teacher," said Derry and, she continued, "when I was at school, I hated maths, but I liked music, nature and animals. I had a pet toad who I brought to school with me daily. Angus the toad as he was called would ride around in my school satchel to reach school and then spend the day in my desk. One day one of the maths textbooks was missing from class and Colonel Snyppe insisted he would search everyone's desks. I protested that it was not a good idea to search my desk and that I didn't have the book anyway but lift the lid of my desk he did..."

"Oh dear," said Emmie.

"Angus leaped up into his face," continued Derry. "I thought the *colonel was going to faint. He yelled at me to 'kill that thing' but by then Angus had hopped away and hidden. I was terribly worried about him, but I managed to retrieve him later. He had wisely hidden in the dark of the shoe lockers. It took me ages to find him. I never took him to school again and returned him to the hedge in our garden which had been his original home. I think I learned that there are places where certain creatures should not go."*

"You must have been in trouble," said Emmie.

"I was," said Derry, "but my punishment only made things worse. The Headmistress and Assistant Head each had corgis of indifferent temper who spent their time in the Heads' office. As punishment I was sentenced to not be allowed to share break-time in the grounds or hall with the other pupils for a whole fortnight, but instead I was required to walk the dogs. Well, they were not very obedient. One break-time they dashed away from me... I think they could smell bacon sandwiches in the staff room (sorry Patrick). They pushed the double doors open only to be confronted by Colonel Snyppe holding a bacon sandwich. There was sort of contretemps since I think they were after the bacon, and he got slightly nipped by each dog!"

I listened intently as she finished her story, "Of course there was little he could do as these were the Heads' dogs. But I think he hates smaller animals, possibly all animals. I don't think he has figured out who I am because I use my married name now... and all that at school was twenty-nine years ago when I was twelve."

I don't think I understood all the story, but I think I got the gist of it. I was glad I never had to go to school. It sounded most unpleasant.

"Oink... you like animals a lot," I observed. "You never got bitten by any of these dogs?"

"Well, occasionally by the corgis and other family pets," said Derry. "But I know the difference between a warning nip and a nasty

~ 76 ~

bite. Because somehow, since I knew the difference, I still liked dogs… well, and animals generally."

"How did you become involved in animal rescue?" I asked.

"When I was a young woman, I started to train to be a musician, either to play the cello in an orchestra or be a music teacher. Unfortunately, I had an accident and injured my back and arm when I fell off a moped. I was in the course of recovering but I was not fit to resume my studies at music college, so I took a part-time job as a receptionist at a free veterinary clinic, and I learned a great deal about the misfortunes of animals," she replied. Then she continued, "I recall all sorts of incidents like a smartly dressed lady who wanted a kitten put to sleep because the little cat did not match her coat. I remember a vegan man who wondered why his Jack Russell did not thrive when he tried to feed him a diet of pineapple and bananas. Then there was the family who had a hen with a bad leg… she had been kept on the balcony of a fourth floor flat and had to try to fly off it… only to land with bang on the ground since she was not used to flying from that height."

"Did you ever go back to your music?" asked Emmie.

"Eventually," said Derry. "I was never good enough to perform but I did teach cello and violin part-time when Terry started school, because by the time I got my qualification I had got married and had a child."

I grunted. "Do you know anything about pigs?"

"A little, my daughter Terry knows more being a veterinary nurse," she said. "My late father supplied veterinary products to farmers, so we frequently went to agricultural shows when I was a child. At our last house I kept a Vietnamese pot-bellied pig for about 6 months at the end of our garden until he was rehomed at a petting zoo… I think my neighbours were on the cusp of complaining. It was not as unsuitable as *some flat or townhouse since we had a decent sized garden with an old pig-stye in it, but it was too urban. When the house was built in Victorian times no doubt people generally kept a few hens or a pig at the bottom of the garden, but times have changed."*

Then Derry turned to Emmie, "One of the reasons we moved to Granary Manor was because of the space it has outside and its suitability to house some animals in its grounds. I do wish people would understand that I just want to run a small animal rescue centre, not some huge commercial kennels."

Emmie replied, "Unfortunately, you will just need to let the planning processes take their course... gaining a view from the Parish Council is just one facet of the process, although a supporting view from one's Parish Council helps."

I grunted again and inquired, "Do you have any animals now?"

Derry replied, "Three rescue dogs, four rescue cats, three rescue rabbits, two guinea pigs and half a dozen hens."

At this point Delores interrupted with a little squeal, "You like hear pig sing?" she asked.

Derry said, "Yes," and I gleaned from Delores' grunts she wanted to sing 'Walk on By'. I put on the track by Isaac Hayes using my voice control. Within a few minutes she was singing along to the track, but Derry and Emmie seemed to be laughing and giggling.

After the track finished Delores looked very cross and said, "Why you laugh?" with a grunt.

Emmie said, "I'm sorry, Delores. We didn't mean to offend you, but it did sound like 'Pork on By'."

Delores made a dejected grunt and hid her face in a heap of straw. Delores understood human humour even less than me. I would let her have the pick of any vegetable they had left with us as a treat, to cheer her up.

Derry and Emmie left, and I began to think about the needs of ill-treated animals. If a farmer kept one for sausages and looked after one properly until that fateful day, that was one thing, but if a silly person tried to keep a pig as a pet in a very small place, like one of these flat places with not enough food I thought that was worthy of a lot of grunting. Better to have had a shorter but happy life and become sausages than lead a long life of misery. I thought about Derry's wish to save animals from bad conditions. Surely people on the Parish Council should support her.

Part 2

Why does he get into trouble?

I pondered from time to time why Patrick White seemed to get into trouble. Could it be his huge curiosity about how the human world worked? I was pleased that Delores' interest in human matters was more limited. However, I immersed myself in my legal work, taking an interest in local issues. Letitia had moved home from university and was soon to start her professional exam course. In the meanwhile, she had taken herself on a short holiday, visiting Alain's parents in France.

After Derry's visit for advice, I decided I would attend the first Parish Council Meeting after the election. I knew my mother would also be pleased if I attended. I made my way to the village hall for the Parish Council meeting one fine evening. I took my seat with other members of the public next to Derry and Terry. Sven Mossesson was also there as well as Simon Christianson and Jim Birkshaw and a couple of other villagers, most of whom were interested in planning matters being considered tonight by the Parish Council. Alain was away again and none of the children were at home. It was a little early than the time indicated for the meeting, so I took the opportunity to survey the scene.

Colonel Snyppe was present as was the Parish Clerk Benjamina de Hotote. This time she was wearing a bright orange knitted hat with what looked like a macaw made of felt ornamenting the top. She had a huge matching orange knitted jacket which hung down to her knees which she pulled round her. Rebecca was present and I looked out for some of the councillors she had mentioned. There was a local optician Mr Oxtable (who looked very serious), a retired woman police officer Dilly Noble (who had about 6 inches of pancake make-up and a lot of eyeshadow), Manny Sharma from our local village shop (always a smile on his face whatever the situation), and local book-keeper Candy Drydale (who looked very mousy). Until more recent times I had not taken a great deal of notice of Rebecca's Parish Council work. The Parish Councillors were of course volunteers who gave up their time for the good of the community. Most of them had their hearts in the right places, although it did appear that perhaps Colonel Snyppe was getting a little too old for the work and was possibly allowing himself to be influenced by historic prejudices. I didn't want to be ageist, but I understood he was well into his eighties. It appeared he had had three "careers", first as an army officer, then as a maths teacher and more recently as Chairman of the Parish Council.

The Parish Councillors were presenting their paperwork to the Clerk. I understood from Rebecca they needed to do things like complete declaration of interest forms before they could take up their seats. The Village Hall had an odd musty smell about it, befitting some of the people and the atmosphere.

The members of the public were mostly discussing planning matters amongst themselves as they waited. I saw some people who I understood were new to the village, the Kovalenkos who I believed had come to England as refugees from Ukraine and were now settling in our village. They were chatting quietly to Sven Mossesson who looked very dapper and was clutching a clipboard which seemed I presumed to hold a copy of the planning application to convert land at Granary Manor to an animal rescue centre.

Simon Christianson was wearing a dark T-shirt which on one side said, 'The Republic of Aston Villa' and on the other side said, 'Always a Brummie'. I was unclear if he was present for a particular purpose or just for general interest. Colonel Snyppe and Simon Christianson seemed to be eyeing each other up. Colonel Snyppe looked down from the stage and called to him,

"You... yes you there."

Simon said, "Yes," and glared back at the colonel.

"We will not be singing the National Anthem today," said Colonel Snyppe, "but make no mistake we will sing it on important royal occasions, Mr Republican."

Simon Christianson started to say something, but the Clerk was hissing at the colonel. Mr and Mrs Kovalenko looked understandably puzzled. I felt Benjamina had a lot with which to contend. There was still five minutes to go. I could just about make out thunder clouds massing through the church-like windows of the hall. I had a sense of foreboding.

"Before we start," said Benjamina de Hotote, "I have had declarations of interest and other relevant papers from all prospective Parish Councillors except one. And he does not seem to be here. If he does not appear in the next couple of minutes, he will not be able to take up his seat. Does anyone know anything about Patrick White?"

I felt my heart sink and a shiver run down my spine. Surely this could not be my Patrick White. Surely there was not another Patrick White in the village?

There was a loud rumble of thunder and a flash of lightening. The double doors into the hall were pushed wide open. There in the doorway stood an enormous pig with some papers in his mouth which fell to the floor when he opened it to speak.

"Here I am. I'm Patrick White," he said. "Sorry if I am late."

Chapter 7

Humans are very strange

*A*fter giving matters a great deal of thought I decided I ought to go to the Parish Council myself. It seemed to me that there were some people who really did not understand the needs of animals. Personally, if a toad had hopped out at me, I would doubtless have eaten it, but I had a lot of time for the dogs I knew. Piecrust, Emmie's dog always wagged his tail when he saw me and sometimes, he brought me a dog biscuit. Rebecca's dog Selwyn would sit quietly in my shed when he visited. Even Delores who was newer to my arrangements was not upset by them. I surmised there were probably good dogs and bad dogs just as I had discovered there were good and bad humans.

I got on well enough with the farm cats, Empress, Duchess and Princess. They sometimes went mousing in my quarters. I thought this was a good thing. I couldn't see why humans would dislike an animal rescue centre. That being said I had heard some so-called learned humans talking on the television about something called "the drive to net zero." They said we animals caused emissions. They were babbling on the television about both emissions, and something called diversity and needing a commission to investigate the needs of both in low lying islands.

Well, I know some humans find pigs smelly, but really!! The activists wanted to do away with farm animals and pets. I did not think it kind to make us farm pigs either have to survive in the wild or go extinct. As for pets it seemed to do humans good to have animals around them. Some dogs even helped blind humans find their way.

Anyway, I waited until Emmie had gone out and I made sure Delores understood I would come back later. I let myself out quietly and trotted out towards the Village Hall. The weather seemed rather stormy, and I hoped I would not get the papers wet. There was thunder rolling when I pushed open the door. My papers fell down as I apologised for being late. I was surprised by how upset the humans seemed about my presence.

In front of me there were some rows of seats. I could see Emmie sitting there as well as Jim Birkshaw. I also recognised Derry and her husband Sven. Their daughter Terry was sitting with them.

In front of the members of the public was a desk and sitting at the desk was a lady in a silly hat with sticking out teeth, who I understood was Benjamina de Hotote the Parish Council Clerk. Just behind her was a slightly raised area where I could see the humans who I believed were Parish Councillors because Rebecca was sitting amongst them. There was also a pompous looking old man who I understood from what I had been told by Rebecca in the past was Colonel Snyppe. He did not have much hair on his head which I understood was not unusual for older humans.

Initially after I entered and gave my apologies there was a few seconds' silence. Then a woman with blonde hair on the stage started screaming,

"There's a pig, there's a pig."

Actually, it was more like squealing.

I responded, "Madam, oink, I am not just 'a pig'. I am Patrick

White, and I have come about the Parish Council. My name is I believe on the list."

She continued squealing. The colonel was shouting, "Why are there noises like words coming out of that dirty thing...? Get it out of here."

Rebecca intervened, "Madam Clerk... fellow Parish Councillors this is Patrick White the talking pig. You may have seen him on social media. He lives at my daughter's smallholding. He is quite harmless... but I don't know why he is here."

She looked over to Emmie. "Emmie?" she said.

Emmie was standing up and staring at me with a bright red face, "What on earth are you doing here?" she said to me.

I said with a grunt, "Some young people put my name forward to be a Parish Councillor and I believe I was unopposed. I have come to be a Parish Councillor... I have even brought the declaration of interest forms... oink." I could see Emmie looking embarrassed, presumably about Aaron and Charlie's actions and I started to have a few misgivings.

The colonel was shouting, "A dirty smelly pig can't be on the Council."

I replied quietly, "I am not dirty or smelly... I have a daily bath which I am not sure all humans do."

Jim Birkshaw stood up and cleared his throat. "With your permission I would like to speak." Benjamina de Hotote spoke at this point,

"At least someone has some manners!" she said. "We have not formally begun the meeting, but as Parish Clerk someone needs to take control... so please Mr Birkshaw continue..."

Jim cleared his throat, "I know this pig. He was born on my farm. He will not hurt anyone here. He can speak... I even had him brought to a court dispute to demonstrate pig behaviour. I suggest people calm down... I can ask one of my men to bring an animal trailer here if need be, and to take him back to Emmie's place..."

Emmie put up her hand.

"Yes," said the Clerk.

"Patrick White is one of my pigs," said Emmie. "But I did not arrange to bring him here nor did I arrange for his name to be on any papers. It causes me huge embarrassment for him to be here. However, he is remarkable and although I am embarrassed and upset by his presence here tonight, I would plead that no-one panics... he is very interested in the human world... I am sure he can be taken home shortly... and I can give reassurances for the future..."

I grunted and said, "Please can I speak... oink?"

The Clerk nodded.

"I should not... oink... I think have allowed some young people to put my name forward. I really did not want to upset Emmie and Rebecca, but I want the best interests of animals to be considered... as I am able to speak, I thought I could give the welfare of animals a voice. It's not just farm animals, but pet animals. I don't think though some animals like elephants or hippos live locally so I am not talking about them," I spoke.

Colonel Snyppe butted into the conversation,

"It's just a pig," he said. "The Parish Council is for humans not for animals... best place for that thing is on my plate."

One of the other Parish Councillors interrupted,

"Madam Clerk... can I speak please?"

The Clerk nodded. "I am Councillor Candy Drydale," said a rather pale lady. "You may know me from previous times on the Parish Council or been aware that I am the bookkeeper for the butcher's shop in town. I really like cats and dogs, and I have every respect for farmers who have good welfare standards. I am not sure there is any law against an animal being on the Town Council. I have seen Patrick White on social media, and I think it is very brave of Patrick pig for wanting to contribute."

A serious looking man amongst the Councillors put up his hand.

"Councillor Oxtable?" said the Clerk.

"I don't know what the rules are," he said. "We should try to obey the rules if we can, but I also don't want anyone to get into trouble. It seems like someone has wrongly thought we could have a pig on the Council... I doubt we can, but I have no objection to him staying briefly if no-one is in any danger."

"Hang, draw and quarter the lot of them," said the colonel interrupting. "Turn the pig into chops and string up the humans who allowed his name on the papers."

There was uproar again at this point with a man I later learned was called Simon interrupting. I found him hard to understand since he had what is called a Brummie accent, with which I was not familiar. He did seem to be on my side. He was shouting at the colonel.

"Let the pig on the Council... at least he is on the side of something positive... You don't seem to like Brummies or Republicans... Shame on you if you are against animal welfare too..."

There were mixed cries of, "Hear, hear," and "boo."

Sven Mossesson put up his hand. The Clerk indicated he could speak.

"I would not like anyone to get into trouble, and I can understand if rules are important. I hope there is some way we can respect that Patrick White has views too."

The colonel boomed, "Well what are the rules?" he asked looking at the Clerk.

The Clerk cleared her throat.

"I am not sure there is a rule specifically forbidding pigs on Parish Councils." She paused and looked at me. *"Are you over eighteen years of age?"* she asked me.

I grunted, *"Eh... no."*

"I am afraid that disqualifies Mr White from being on the Parish Council," she said. *"However, I can see very little point in making matters worse by referring matters for investigation about election irregularities... I think it would just make the Council look stupid. Now, if you don't mind, I think in a couple of minutes we should start the meeting."*

"What about the pig?" boomed the colonel.

"I want to hear from the pig," shouted Simon. The Clerk seemed to pretend she did not hear him.

"I would suggest," said the Clerk, *"he can stay... if he behaves. There is a section when members of the public are allowed to speak. He might want to give a view then. After that... he and his supporters might want to get him home."*

The colonel scowled.

A man I learned to be Manny Sharma put up a hand to attract attention and Benjamina nodded towards him, but the colonel butted in before he could speak.

"Do you mind," said the colonel, *"I am the Chairman of the Parish Council. I should be saying who speaks. I think we should get rid of the pig and that's that."*

Benjamina retorted, *"You were the Chairman for the last annual period, but the formal Council meeting has not begun, let alone voting for the Chairman. I think we should let Mr Sharma speak."*

There was a general sound of *"yesses."* Mr Sharma cleared his throat.

"My name is Mr Manny Sharma, and I am your local shop owner,

and I also sit on the Parish Council. As some of you may know I am a Hindu. Amongst Hindu Gods there are pig gods. We respect animals in my religion. It is a very unique situation we are in... we should not be making rash decisions and assume we cannot learn from this experience. I have also seen Patrick the pig on social media... I do not fear him. Let him stay as long as the rest of the public."

"Oink. Thank you," I interjected.

The man called Simon was calling out, "Let the pig stay."

The Clerk said quietly and firmly,

"Will everyone be quiet. It is time the Council meeting started. I suggest the Parish Council begins and votes its Chairman and Vice Chairman and if the Councillors wish they can take a vote as to whether the pig stays or leaves."

There was nodding amongst the Councillors. I was a bit sad I could not take part. I thought I would have made a good Chairman. I imagined myself grunting loudly to keep people in order. The meeting formally started, and I think to the colonel's surprise the Councillors chose Mr Sharma to be Chairman, and the colonel as Vice Chairman. The colonel looked rather cross.

Mr Sharma said, "I think one of our first items of business is whether the pig can stay."

"I have to declare an interest," said Rebecca, "as Patrick White lives at my daughter's place."

The Clerk said, "Best if you do not vote then."

Councillor Drydale said, "I would like to propose that the pig is allowed to stay as long as the public are allowed to stay, and provided Mrs Martyns and Mr Birkshaw remain as well."

Councillor Oxtable said he seconded the motion. The colonel who had gone a very odd colour kept saying, "Disgrace, disgrace," under his breath. When there was a vote Rebecca did not take part and *everyone else except Rebecca and the colonel put up their hands in favour of me staying.*

We soon got to the part where members of the public were allowed to speak. Simon started waving his hand furiously.

"Yes, Mr Christianson," said Mr Sharma.

"My name is Simon Christianson and I'm a Republican," he began. "But I'm not here this time because of that... I am here because I want to highlight climate change... and also support the Mossessons' planning application. It's a good idea if there is an animal rescue centre there... at Granary Manor. As long as it's environmentally friendly, mind. People use fossil fuels and cars far too much. I wanted to highlight my concern to the Council about what we are doing to the environment."

Mr Mossesson put up his hand. "May I be allowed to speak?" Mr Sharma nodded.

He continued, "Granary Manor is well away from its nearest neighbours. It has plenty of land to accommodate what is planned. My wife who is the driving force plans accommodation for ten cats, ten dogs and animal sheds and mini paddocks for up to eight larger animals such as goats or pigs with a hen house and run for maybe a dozen birds. As to the environmental question, solar panels are planned on some of the roofs of buildings to help with costs."

Derry put up her hand and was able to add, "This is not a commercial enterprise, so I have no intention of having vast numbers of animals. I will be reliant on charitable donations to run it. In fact, I am hoping Patrick White will do a little film for me on social media, singing a song."

I could hear the colonel saying, "Piffle," in the background. I decided to grunt loudly and say, "Can I say something from... oink... an animal's point of view?"

"Yes, of course," said Mr Sharma. The colonel seemed to have turned a funny colour.

I began, "Oink, as you know my name is Patrick White and I am a pig. I can talk and read and write too. I watch the news and go online. Oink. You humans are a funny lot. Humans claim to be animal lovers..."

The colonel interrupted under his breath, "Well I don't love them." I ignored him and continued.

"Humans claim to be animal lovers, but many people don't have a clue how to look after animals. I think it is a good thing... oink, oink, if there is a local animal rescue centre. I visited a big town once. It would be terrible to be a pig in a flat in a town. Most farmers look after pigs well because they know we taste better if we have been happy and healthy. I have dog and cat companions. I know they eat a lot so some people can't always manage to feed them, so they need to have a place too... in case oink... something goes wrong. My people seem to be always feeding the cats... I don't know if it's because they are rich or the cats are greedy, but I hear other folks can't always manage so well... oink oink oink. And this environment bit, if humans put their planet first, wouldn't they stop invading each other's land and trying to blow each other up rather than having 'stop oil' protests... oink... I am sure these solar panel things will be useful though... oink oink, unless they put them where they grow turnips and potatoes."

I stopped there. To my pleasure and surprise there was a round of applause from the members of the public. I bowed my head in acknowledgment and then lay down just behind the seating for members of the public.

Mr Sharma checked that no more members of the public wished to speak and then the Parish Council went on to discuss a lot of things which, for a pig, seemed rather boring but to humans were obviously important. Eventually they reached the planning application for there to be an Animal Rescue Centre at Granary Manor. There was a spirited debate between the Parish Councillors, with Mr Sharma chairing the discussion in a firm but polite way despite Colonel Snyppe trying to interrupt and take over from time to time. After quite a heated discussion with Colonel Snyppe making his opposition very clear, the Parish Council voted to support the planning application.

Sven and Derry and Terry quietly left after hearing the decision. The meeting continued.

Mr Sharma cleared his throat,

"There is next an Agenda item to form a working group to promote and preserve the countryside within our Parish boundaries. I think we are looking for both Parish Councillors and volunteers from members of the public. Let us see who is interested on the Council?"

Rebecca asked to be included as did Councillors Drydale and Oxtable.

"Any members of the public like to volunteer today?" added Mr Sharma.

Simon Christianson put his hand-up. "I'd like to volunteer," he said in his broad Brummie accent, "and I wonder if we shouldn't ask the pig?"

"You can't ask the pig," boomed out the colonel.

"If I ask the pig," said Mr Sharma, "it will be because it is the right thing to do, so be quiet. I think subject to any advice from the Clerk we should have a vote. Working Groups don't have to meet in the Village Hall so I myself can't see a problem with practicalities."

The Clerk indicated she advised there was no reason why there should not be a vote.

The Parish Councillors voted that by a narrow majority I should be on the working group.

Colonel Snyppe got up with a face which looked as dark maroon as any beetroot. He strode to the door and walked out.

"Oh, dear," said Mr Sharma, but no other comment was made.

The meeting soon drew to a close. Rebecca, Emmie and Jim Birkshaw were chatting to me as to whether I could just walk home.

"I've already sent a text to my bloke Greg to have him on standby, Emmie," said Jim. "So, no need to get your trailer out."

"Oink. I could walk," I said.

"What! And get into more trouble," said Emmie. "In the nicest possible way, Patrick, you really are a trial to me!"

Jim said he was sending a text to Greg to get him down to the Hall urgently.

Mr Kovalenko came up to us.

"I came to see how the Parish Council worked," he said. "Are they always this interesting?"

Chapter 8

(i)   How mock is a Trial

Afarfter Patrick managed to get himself tangled up in Parish politics, I tried to re-introduce him to a more piggy way of life. He was briefly put in a paddock with a sow for the purpose of producing more piglets but professed his preference to return to Delores and his comforts after he had his wicked way with the sow. I toyed again with putting a big padlock on the bolt to the door to his quarters but dismissed the idea. By the time he had broken it and gone out somewhere he would be long out of my reach. In the end I had my tame electrician rig up a sounder alarm which meant that every time anyone went in and out of the door a 'bing-bong' could be heard. I was sure I would hear that in the quiet of the small hours.

Patrick was not pleased.

"Don't you trust me?" he grunted.

"Not entirely," I replied.

"Derry and Terry like me," he retorted.

"That is as maybe," I said. "But I can't have you wandering the neighbourhood. Anyway, another of your fans Jake Daniels is coming to go over the mock trial arrangements with us."

As if I needed the mock trial! In reality, I had my hands full with real legal work, the small holding and running the house. Alain and I didn't even have time for a proper holiday this summer, just managing a whirlwind city break in Budapest for four nights. However, having agreed to the mock trial I could not see how I could get out of things now. Also, I felt Jake Daniels was a better influence on Patrick than say Charlie Catton, whose presence was not particularly welcome these days after the trouble he had initiated. Patrick was certainly a popular pig. As well as his usual visits from my mother Rebecca, he now had visits from Derry and Terry and Jake Daniels on a regular basis. When Mr and Mrs Kovalenko came to see me about making wills they asked for a quick visit to Patrick as well. Patrick was fortunately on his best behaviour. He greeted them politely and did not say anything embarrassing. He sang a few stanzas of Rick Astley's 'Never Gonna Give You up' which he had recently added to his repertoire.

Delores took Patrick's visitors all in her stride and had struck up a bit of a rapport with Jake. She would come to him each time he visited to have her ears scratched. I asked Jake about all the time he was spending with the pigs.

"Don't you want to spend more time with the other students?" I asked.

"They are all dispersed for the summer vacation," he said. "Besides, I want to do a good job, and I am enjoying getting out of town... it makes a change from student and urban life."

I didn't press him further. Nor did I think Patrick pressed him. It appeared they had spent their time in serious conversation in preparation for the mock trial. Unlike a real-life trial Jake had been involved in all the trial paper preparations. At the time he prepared most of the papers he did not know if he would be prosecution or defence counsel, and the twist was it had only been confirmed later he would play defence counsel. As to his client, he was of course a bit different to most defendants. I understood prosecution Counsel was to be played by a university lecturer who was Deputy to the Dean of the Law Faculty, an Assistant Professor, and part-time Barrister Jonathan Billius, rather than a student. Jonathan Bilius had not been let into the secret of who the real defendant might be. I could not say I knew him, although I vaguely remembered him from some local legal practitioners' meeting. He was as I recalled quite a short man with a high opinion of himself, who had over the years got himself on various legal consultative groups. I was given to understand by Jake he didn't really see eye to eye with His Honour, but there was no open animosity. It seemed from the little Jake had said he coveted the revered status of His Honour Judge Armstrong KC. He was second in command to the Head of Faculty but apparently saw himself as more important than he really was.

I mentioned Jonathan Bilius to Alain. He guffawed.

"That prat," he said. "He richly deserves to find he is prosecuting a pig… I've come across him at Circuit meetings, always trying to get on whatever committee seemed important… always full of his own importance telling us he was an Assistant Professor as well as a barrister. I remember him boasting about his daughters as well. How one daughter was apparently a famous ballet dancer and the other going to study English lit at Oxford. I tried to speak to him since I thought we had something in common with daughters in a similar age group. He was very dismissive as if I was a smell under his nose." He paused. "I learned later his daughter was in the 'corps de ballet'… in other words just the general company, although talented, I'm sure. The bloke suffers from 'small man syndrome'. You know if someone approached him to serve on a Royal Commission for pompous prats he would probably accept."

"That's a bit harsh," I said, and Patrick interrupted to ask what 'small man syndrome' meant.

I replied, "As you know, Patrick, humans come in all shapes and sizes. Some mean humans think that occasionally some short men compensate for their lack of height by becoming... well... I suppose super pompous and thinking they are more important than they really are."

Alain laughed and Patrick grunted. It was not often that Alain took against someone in that way or that he was indeed prejudiced against people of small stature.

I talked to Jake about the practical arrangements for the day of the trial which was fast approaching. It appeared I would need to go ahead of Scuffy who would drive the trailer. I was worried in case they stopped anywhere. I didn't want Patrick to start chatting to people. Rebecca couldn't really travel with Patrick either. Letitia was to hold the fort at my little legal office at the farm since my work from the locals had taken an upturn. Terry fortunately came to the rescue as I happened to mention my concerns.

"I am trained as a veterinary nurse, so I have no qualms about actually riding with Patrick in his trailer. I'll take the day off work. I am sure Patrick won't harm me," she said when we were chatting one day.

"But Patrick is an enormous boar..." I responded. "Won't you get squashed?"

"Put a big hay bale in," said Terry. "I'll sit behind that."

Although I had some reservations, I decided to take up Terry's offer. I also decided to arm Terry with a large bucket of apples and carrots and a flagon of water behind her bale. Terry brought her own Thermos of coffee with her and didn't seem at all bothered about things.

Rebecca and I travelled together to the University lecture theatre. I felt reassured by arrangements. It was a lovely sunny autumn day. I had provided Scuffy and Terry with full instructions and lectured Patrick about being on his best behaviour. When we arrived, I took my place at a table to play Judge's Clerk. I was introduced to a young girl from amongst the students who said she was called Anna and would be the court usher. I set my laptop up. Rebecca took her place with the students who were playing the witnesses. I saw Jake Daniels fleetingly. Jonathan Bilius was there with a timid looking lad who was apparently assisting him. The rest of the law students were on the curved benches of the lecture theatre.

I didn't know if it was my imagination but after a while, I thought I could just make out the engine of Scuffy's truck and a slight grunting noise.

The lecture theatre had a stage which went straight across the back. At one side furniture had been arranged for His Honour Judge Armstong KC and there was a label on the desk saying, 'Judge'. In the middle of the stage was a lectern to which a label, 'witness' had been affixed. This left a fair amount of space. One lonely looking chair with the label, 'defendant' had been placed there. I was sure the students had no clue that the defendant would not be sitting on the chair. There were doors to the outside world in the wings to the side of the stage. On one side there was also a dressing room area behind the wings where I suspected His Honour had been secreted but on the other side large doors led out to the playing field area. On the back wall there was a screen where I understood His Honour intended that I display the witness statements with Anna's help.

Anna approached me because there was an expectant hush and Jonathan Bilius and Jake Daniels had taken their places. Dressed in wigs and gowns as befitted prosecution and defence Counsel each had a laptop on the table in front of them.

"Mrs Martyns I am told the defendant is here and His Honour is ready," she said.

I stood up and cleared my throat. "Silence in Court," I said loudly. "Please stand for His Honour Judge Armstrong KC."

His Honour came in and Jake and Jonathan bowed slightly to him as did Jonathan's assistant and Anna. I nodded my head slightly. There was shuffling from the students' seats. Keeping to my role I announced,

"The Crown against Patrick White. Does Your Honour want the defendant in yet?"

"In a few minutes, Mrs Martyns," said His Honour. "But first I have a few words for you all." He looked at the students.

"You are all jurors today. This is an unusual trial which I hope will help prepare you for the surprises life presents. Counsel for the Prosecution and for the Defence... I trust you will maintain professional decorum at all times. Now, Mrs Martyns I think you can send your usher out... stage left. To collect the defendant!"

I indicated to Anna to go out through the wings toward the playing field.

She returned a couple of minutes later ashen faced followed by Patrick flanked by Scuffy and Terry.

"There's a pig, a pig," she cried out.

"That's right," said His Honour. "Patrick White is a pig."

"Oink," said Patrick. "Of course, I am. Doesn't anyone... oink... look at social media? I am a famous pig."

(ii) *How Mock is a Trial*

The ride in the back of the trailer was relatively short and Terry chatted to me quite a lot. She asked me questions about my likes and dislikes. I think if the journey had been much longer it would have become rather irritating, but for the short distance I found it reassuring. When the trailer was pulled to a stop, I heard Scuffy call out,

"We are here now... best behaviour!"

As he opened the trailer door Terry proffered some water and a carrot. I accepted these readily and looked out at my surroundings. We were on a small concrete area next to a building by a big green grassy field which had some post things I believe humans use for football. There was a small flower bed with some thorny bushes next to the field.

"I need to go," I said to Scuffy and Terry.

"You aint going walkabout," said Scuffy.

"No... grunt... do my business before we go inside," I explained.

"Well try the flowerbed... I don't think they want pig doings in the middle of the field."

I trotted out and edged towards the flowerbed, but it was too small and full of thorns, so I quickly took myself to the area where the posts were.

"Oh dear," said Terry.

"Back of the net... a goal I'd say," said Scuffy of the offering I had left at the back of the football goal.

I didn't quite understand what he meant, and I sat myself down next to the trailer. It wasn't long before a door in the building opened, and a young girl with a clipboard in her hand came outside.

"I'm looking for Patrick White," she said. "I am the court usher today."

"Oink... here I am," I replied.

"You're a pig," she said, and hurried back into the building followed by Terry, Scuffy and I. Within a few seconds I found myself on a stage. I could see the Judge at his seat, and I spotted Emmie and Jake. There was a short man with a pink face who I assumed was Jonathan Bilius. There were rows of seats in a semi-circle going up several levels. They were filled with young humans. For a moment I was reminded of a human history picture of a gladiator going into a Roman amphitheatre and I don't mind saying I was a bit nervous. The young girl was saying, "There's a pig, a pig."

"That's right," said His Honour. "Patrick White is a pig."

"Oink," said I. "Of course, I am... doesn't anyone... oink... look at social media? I am a famous pig."

There was laughter and comments from the young humans, but eventually Emmie wrapped her knuckles on the table and said very loudly,

"Silence in court. Do not interrupt His Honour. Any further disturbance and those causing it will be ejected."

"Indeed," said His Honour. "But I would rather that did not happen as you the student audience are the jury. This trial will proceed as any other trial. The only difference is the defendant is a pig. This is an object lesson in dealing with the unexpected and getting over your prejudices."

"Your Honour," said Jonathan Bilius looking pink in the face. "Might I be permitted to address you?"

His Honour said, "Yes, Mr Bilius."

"I was not made aware that you were bringing a pig into the lecture theatre, surely you cannot have permission?"

His Honour looked Mr Bilius in the eye,

"'Surely you cannot have permission, Your Honour?'," said the Judge emphasizing the words 'Your Honour' which had been omitted, and continuing, "I have notified the Dean an animal would be brought into the lecture theatre, and he had no objection."

"But presumably not a pig, Your Honour?" queried Bilius.

"Well, I didn't specify," said the Judge.

"So, Your Honour, in effect you have just done your own thing... declared UDI! I must protest," said Bilius looking puffed up like one of Emmie's bantam cockerels.

"Well," said His Honour, "maybe I have... but I am the one running this mock trial not you! As I said today is all about dealing with the unexpected and getting over prejudices. Let us proceed."

Bilius looked very angry. Jake looked rather nervous. Emmie looked concerned. The Judge had a big smile across his face. I didn't know how to feel.

Emmie read out the indictment and paused after each section to ask me if I was "Guilty," or "Not Guilty?" To each I replied, "Oink... Not Guilty."

Even though it was a 'pretend' trial it felt all too real. People were staring at me. Everyone looked extremely serious. When Jonathan Bilius gave his opening speech, it sounded very effective although it was obvious the Patrick White to whom he referred sounded like a person and he gave me a stare of pure hatred. When he began calling his witnesses this look did not go from his face. He made me feel very uncomfortable even though I knew the trial was a pretence.

The witnesses apart from Rebecca were played by students, but they had all tried to dress up in costumes to match their roles. Mr Bilius was surprisingly loud and repetitive. Whereas Jake took a much calmer approach. His gentle cross examination seemed quite effective.

The student playing Mr Apples had dressed himself in a tweed suit with a big scarf and he wore a hat like I had seen in a Sherlock Holmes film on television. He was obviously putting on an odd plummy voice. Jake firstly got him to admit the windfalls on the *ground were not in a good state and past their best. Then, Jake gently cross-examined him as to whether it was a hazardous thing to do to try and take an apple out of a pig's mouth. He said,*

"Couldn't the words saying that you shouldn't put your hand there just have been a suggestion that you might get hurt accidentally rather than a threat?"

"That is one way of looking at it," pretend Mr Apples replied.

"Would you have tried to take an apple out of a human's mouth?" persisted Jake.

Fake Mr Apples was now confused as he had presumably rehearsed on the basis the defendant was a human,

"I had thought he was..." he blurted out. "I mean... well it wasn't his apple." The students sniggered.

Jake had made his point.

Jake asked few questions of Mr Barley Mow. The student playing him had dressed himself in some sort of shepherd's outfit including a white smock and a battered wide brimmed straw hat. He took off the hat as he took his place and pieces straw flew out of it.

Jake asked him,

"You never saw Patrick White bite Mr Apples, did you?"

The answer was of course, "No."

"You saw the boss waving a tree branch at Mr White, didn't you?"

"Yes," was the reply, and Jake continued,

"But you didn't see Mr White being aggressive, did you?"

"'Spose not," was the answer followed by a bout of coughing probably brought on by the bits of straw in the air. Humans seem more easily irritated by that sort of thing than pigs.

I could see Bilius looking cross every time it appeared Jake scored a point.

Jake was able to get the fake police officer (dressed in fake police uniform) to confirm I had been co-operative. The medical witness did not appear as that evidence had been agreed.

His Honour decreed we should take a break before we moved on to the defence evidence. I was glad of the chance to go outside and breathe some fresh air before I gave my evidence. Although I kept reminding myself that it was all 'make-believe' I still felt very nervous. I was particularly worried by Jonathan Bilius, who kept fixing me with a malevolent stare. Although I knew he was only playing a part, and that His Honour liked me, I was still concerned about what he might do in real life. I wished I had never agreed to the mock trial and that I was safe and sound with Delores back at Emmie's little farm at the village of Cobblemarkham. I had a drink of water provided by Terry and braced myself to be cross-examined.

Chapter 9

i.   *The Cross Examination of Patrick White*

Patrick stood on the stage of the Lecture Theatre rather than in a dock. But nonetheless the make-believe trial had a certain strange reality to it. It was Patrick's turn to give evidence. As Clerk I administered the oath and Patrick affirmed and promised to tell the truth. Jake asked Patrick to confirm his statement was true and asked if he had anything to add to his account. Patrick replied with a grunt that he had nothing to add.

I watched Jonathan Bilius stare Patrick in the eye as he readied himself to cross-examine Patrick. He leaned right back in his chair and rocked a little, and I worried it might tip over. Patrick then stared right back. Silence descended on the lecture theatre. Jonathan Bilius stood.

"You," said Jonathan Bilius putting the emphasis on the word 'you'. "Are just a pig."

"I am a pig," replied Patrick. "But not just any pig."

"Pigs don't care whose food they eat," said Bilius.

"Well, it depends," said Patrick defensively. "If the choice was between hen food and your dinner, I would choose your dinner if given a choice... oink..."

"So, you admit you might eat someone else's dinner?" said Bilius triumphantly.

"Oink... so might anyone... in the right circumstances," said Patrick.

"Moving on," said Bilius. "The apples in the orchard were not your apples, were they?"

"If you are referring to apples... oink. Oink on the trees, they were not my apples. But there were apples on the ground... discarded..."

"They had not been discarded, had they? They had just fallen off the trees, so you stole them," pressed Bilius.

"I was hungry," said Patrick. "I just picked up rotten apples off the ground. Many of which had already been got at by birds and insects... but they are not in the dock... oink... are they?"

"But you attacked Mr Apples to retain the fruit," pressed Bilius triumphantly.

Patrick appeared to roll his little piggy eyes and sticking to the script said, "He waved a big stick at me and tried to pull the apples out of my mouth."

"Which you should not have had..." pressed Bilius.

Patrick responded, "Snort... so you say again. The crux of the matter is that I was a hungry pig and there was waste fruit on the ground, Mr Apples was very silly. He got hurt because you don't stick a hand in a pig's mouth. I got chased in a shed. It was all needlessly unpleasant... by the way there were no signs warning against picking up fruit. I do wonder if Mr Apples would have treated a child so badly..."

Bilius said triumphantly, "What good would a sign have done... you are a pig... you can't read..."

Patrick leaned forward and looked Bilius straight in the eye.

"Don't be so silly," said Patrick. "Of course I can read. I read the Financial Times online every day."

Bilius looked furious and a funny sort of purple colour. "Someone has coached you to say that you can read in order to confuse the Court," he pressed, as there were sniggers all around.

"Look... snort... oink," said Patrick. "I know I am playing a part today, but I can genuinely read. If someone puts something on the big screen, I will prove it."

Bilius turned and faced His Honour Judge Armstrong KC,

"If it pleases Your Honour, I would like the opportunity to test this... but can the item put on screen be of my choosing?"

"Within reason, yes," said His Honour. "Do you need the case adjourned for five minutes to find something?"

"No," said Bilius. "I have something in mind already."

He handed a note to me. I sought the assistance of the usher Anna and within a few minutes we had on screen,

"Theft Act 1968

1968 CHAPTER 60

An Act to revise the law of England and Wales as to theft and similar or associated offences, and in connection therewith to make provision as to criminal proceedings by one party to a marriage against the other, and to make certain amendments extending beyond England and Wales in the Post Office Act 1953 and other enactments; and for other purposes connected therewith.

[26th July 1968]

Modifications etc. (not altering text)

C1Act amended as to mode of trial by Magistrates' Courts Act 1980 (c. 43, SIF 82), **Sch. 1 para. 28**

C2By Criminal Justice Act 1991 (c. 53, SIF 39:1), s. 101(1), **Sch. 12 para. 23**; S.I. 1991/2208, art. 2(1), **Sch.1** it is provided (14.10.1991) that in relation to any time before the commencement of s. 70 of that 1991 Act (which came into force on 1.10.1992 by S.I.

1992/333, <u>art. 2(2)</u>, **Sch. 2**) references in any enactment amended by that 1991 Act, to youth courts shall be construed as references to juvenile courts.

Commencement Information

I1Act wholly in force at 1.1.1969, see <u>s. 35(1)</u>

Definition of "theft"

1   Basic definition of theft.

(1)A person is guilty of theft if he dishonestly appropriates property belonging to another with the intention of permanently depriving the other of it; and "thief" and "steal" shall be construed accordingly.

(2)It is immaterial whether the appropriation is made with a view to gain, or is made for the thief's own benefit.

(3)The five following sections of this Act shall have effect as regards the interpretation and operation of this section (and, except as otherwise provided by this Act, shall apply only for purposes of this section).

Modifications etc. (not altering text)

C3S. 1(1) applied (25.8.2000) by <u>2000 c. 6</u>, **ss. 148(8)**, <u>168</u>

2   "Dishonestly"

(1)A person's appropriation of property belonging to another is not to be regarded as dishonest—

(a)if he appropriates the property in the belief that he has in law the right to deprive the other of it, on behalf of himself or of a third person; or

(b)if he appropriates the property in the belief that he would have the other's consent if the other knew of the appropriation and the circumstances of it; or

(c)(except where the property came to him as trustee or personal representative) if he appropriates the property in the belief that the person to whom the property belongs cannot be discovered by taking reasonable steps.

(2)A person's appropriation of property belonging to another may be dishonest notwithstanding that he is willing to pay for the property.

3   "Appropriates."

(1)Any assumption by a person of the rights of an owner amounts to an appropriation, and this includes, where he has come by the property (innocently or not) without stealing it, any later assumption of a right to it by keeping or dealing with it as owner.

(2)Where property or a right or interest in property is or purports to be transferred for value to a person acting in good faith, no later assumption by him of rights which he believed himself to be acquiring shall, by reason of any defect in the transferor's title, amount to theft of the property.

4   "Property."

(1)"Property" includes money and all other property, real or personal, including things in action and other intangible property.

(2)A person cannot steal land, or things forming part of land and severed from it by him or by his directions, except in the following cases, that is to say—

(a)when he is a trustee or personal representative, or is authorised by power of attorney, or as liquidator of a company, or otherwise, to sell or dispose of land belonging to another, and he appropriates the land or anything forming part of it by dealing with it in breach of the confidence reposed in him; or

(b)when he is not in possession of the land and appropriates anything forming part of the land by severing it or causing it to be severed, or after it has been severed; or

(c)when, being in possession of the land under a tenancy, he appropriates the whole or part of any fixture or structure let to be used with the land.

- For purposes of this subsection "land" does not include incorporeal hereditaments; "tenancy" means a tenancy for years or any less period and includes an agreement for such a tenancy, but a person who after the end of a tenancy remains in possession as statutory tenant or otherwise is to be treated as having possession under the tenancy, and "let" shall be construed accordingly.

(3)A person who picks mushrooms growing wild on any land, or who picks flowers, fruit or foliage from a plant growing wild on any land, does not (although not in possession of the land) steal what he picks, unless he does it for reward or for sale or other commercial purpose.

- For purposes of this subsection "mushroom" includes any fungus, and "plant" includes any shrub or tree.

(4)Wild creatures, tamed or untamed, shall be regarded as property; but a person cannot steal a wild creature not tamed nor ordinarily kept in captivity, or the carcase of any such creature, unless either it has been reduced into possession by or on behalf of another person and possession of it has not since been lost or abandoned, or another person is in course of reducing it into possession.

5   "Belonging to another."

(1)Property shall be regarded as belonging to any person having possession or control of it, or having in it any proprietary right or interest (not being an equitable interest arising only from an agreement to transfer or grant an interest).

(2)Where property is subject to a trust, the persons to whom it belongs shall be regarded as including any person having a right to enforce the trust, and an intention to defeat the trust shall be regarded accordingly as an intention to deprive of the property any person having that right.

(3)Where a person receives property from or on account of another, and is under an obligation to the other to retain and deal with that property or its proceeds in a particular way, the property or proceeds shall be regarded (as against him) as belonging to the other.

(4)Where a person gets property by another's mistake, and is under an obligation to make restoration (in whole or in part) of the property or its proceeds or of the value thereof, then to the extent of that obligation the property or proceeds shall be regarded (as against him) as belonging to the person entitled to restoration, and an intention not to make restoration shall be regarded accordingly as an intention to deprive that person of the property or proceeds.

(5)Property of a corporation sole shall be regarded as belonging to the corporation notwithstanding a vacancy in the corporation.

6   "With the intention of permanently depriving the other of it."

(1)A person appropriating property belonging to another without meaning the other permanently to lose the thing itself is nevertheless to be regarded as having the intention of permanently depriving the other of it if his intention is to treat the thing as his own to dispose of regardless of the other's rights; and a borrowing or lending of it may amount to so treating it if, but only if, the borrowing or lending is for a period and in circumstances making it equivalent to an outright taking or disposal.

(2)Without prejudice to the generality of subsection (1) above, where a person, having possession or control (lawfully or not) of property belonging to another, parts with the property under a condition as to its return which he may not be able to perform, this (if done for purposes of his own and without the other's authority) amounts to treating the property as his own to dispose of regardless of the other's rights."

Once it was displayed Bilius said triumphantly,

"There. Read that."

Patrick gave a snort of contempt and started to read the paragraphs of the Theft Act. As he concluded reading the paragraph for 'Appropriates', His Honour intervened,

"Enough," he said.

Bilius looked as if he would explode.

"Do you have any further cross-examination, Mr Bilius?" said His Honour.

Bilius shook his head and mumbled "No, Your Honour."

Patrick was allowed to sit down. Jake called my mother to give her evidence. This did not take very long. Soon we reached closing arguments and His Honour's direction to the jury who were the approximate seventy students in the lecture theatre. He gave his direction in a serious tone of voice, and it seemed to me to be impeccably balanced.

Everyone left the lecture theatre except the students, and Anna who was doubling up as jury bailiff. I went outside. The late afternoon sun was shining. Jake, Rebecca, Scuffy, Terry and Patrick were sitting on the grass. I peeked around the corner, and I could see Bilius pacing up and down the car park. I was not sure where His Honour had gone.

"It is all rather silly," said Patrick. "That man Bilius seems to take it far too seriously… oink… I am not nervous anymore."

I smiled. We had been enjoying the sun for about an hour when Anna reappeared,

"We have a verdict," she said. "His Honour wants everyone back indoors."

We went back inside and resumed our roles.

Taking up my role as Clerk again I asked who the Mock Jury Foreman from the student body was, and a scruffy, freckled young lad of about nineteen stood up. I read each charge on the indictment and to each he replied the finding was, "Not Guilty."

Before he sat down, he cleared his throat. "On behalf of the students I would like to thank His Honour Judge Armstrong KC for putting on such an interesting and fun event... we would also like to thank the truly remarkable Patrick White... the students welcome him here any time."

There were cries of, "Hear, hear,", "Cheers," and a round of applause.

Jonathan Bilius got up suddenly. "I'd like to seek leave to appeal," he yelled.

"Don't be such an ass," said His Honour looking down on him. "It was a mock trial and now it's over."

ii.   The Aftermath of the Trial

I was very pleased to have got the trial out of the way and to get Patrick back home. I let Jake Daniels know he was still welcome to visit my farm. The return journey was uneventful. Things seemed to settle back down. There was legal work to do, and pigs to fatten. Rebecca had her Parish Council work. Letitia seemed to settle into legal practice. For a while Patrick seemed content in the company of Delores. He did not try to get out to wander the neighbourhood. Alain was home for a while since he had a few cases in the local vicinity. By my standards life was relatively normal. Then I got a letter in the post.

The envelope had the crest of the local University and before I opened it, I thought it was from His Honour but that was not the case. It was a letter from Jonathan Bilius written on official notepaper, purporting to be on behalf of the University.

'Dear Mrs Martyns,

I am writing to you as Deputy Head of Faculty. First, I would like to make it clear that I in no way condone animal cruelty. However, I believe the University was tricked into allowing that pig onto its premises and may be entitled to some recompense for the damage it did.

The following day after it's visit there was to be a friendly soccer match on the playing field behind the lecture theatre, being staff v new students. I was playing for the staff team and was asked to play in goal. Imagine my horror when I found myself sliding around in large piles of pig excrement in the back of the goal. The match had to be called off so the field could be cleared of manure by university groundsmen and contractors. I was covered in embarrassment. My football kit had to be thrown away.

I seek from you the modest sum of £1000 compensation for the university and myself. I also ask you never attend on university premises again. Further, I seek an assurance that you will have that animal humanely destroyed within the next 21 days so it cannot cause such damage again. The life it is leading is plainly not suitable for a farm animal. If I do not hear from you that it has been destroyed in that timescale, I will report matters to the RSPCA, the District Council Animal and Environmental Health departments and the Ministry of Agriculture.

Regards J. Bilius.'

My heart sank. Although I did not think there was any case for anything to happen to Patrick, the last thing I wanted was an invasion of officials with unknown consequences. I was not worried about the money, but I did not think Mr Bilius deserved it. I decided not to tell Patrick about the letter straight away. However, I did confer with Alain, Rebecca and Letitia.

We all agreed I should telephone His Honour Judge Armstrong KC. I did so as soon as I was able, catching him just after he rose from court. I read out the letter to him word for word.

"Leave it with me, it is my responsibility to sort this out as I got you to bring Patrick White to the campus," he said. "It's just malicious because Bilius lost... mind you I am sorry I missed him sliding around in pig dung. Don't pay him a penny... I have an idea. If it works Mr Bilius will not be troubling us for quite a while." I wondered what he had in mind.

Since I didn't know what he had in mind so with a heavy heart I decided to tell Patrick about the situation.

Chapter 10

Is there any justice in the world?

I had begun to think that there was some hope for humanity after the students acquitted me. I was pleased to be home with Delores and to my warm and safe quarters. Hopefully, I had pleased Emmie, Rebecca, Terry and young Jake Daniels. I thought I had demonstrated that I had been a good and clever pig. Then Emmie told me of the unpleasant letter from Jonathan Bilius. I could not help thinking that he deserved to be made into sausages. I became worried and had trouble sleeping. I did not want to be taken away. I thought his behaviour was unfair. I wondered if he would have made such a drama if there had been dog dirt in the goal. Delores tried to nuzzle up to me to comfort me, but she didn't really understand.

The weather was becoming quite inclement as October progressed. There were storms with high winds and heavy rain and the weather people called the storms silly names. I could hear the wind whistling outside my barn. One Thursday night a few days after the letter from Jonathan Bilius the weather was particularly bad. In the early hours of the morning, I heard a sort of cracking noise. The power to my television, computer and electric light went off. I slid back the bolt to the door and pushed it open to see what was happening. The chime on *the door did not sound so I assumed Emmie could not hear me. Indeed, the house seemed to be in darkness. I heard Alain and Emmie's voices going on about, "bloody power cut" and "sodding storm", so I figured they were alright. I decided this might be the chance to go on a little walk. I told Delores to stay indoors. I think she was nervous of the high winds anyway.*

I walked cautiously down the drive and as I went out into the lane, I saw that a big branch had fallen off a tree and was dangling on some cable things, part of which were now hanging down. There were sparks flying so I thought I had better keep away from them. Humans did have such odd contraptions. I was not sure what this one did.

I began to walk towards the village. As I approached the village, I noticed it was very dark. Nowhere had their lights on. From time to time the wind swirled blowing up banks of leaves which seemed to eddy and rise almost in the same way as murmurations of starlings. There was a fallen tree in the road, partly blocking it, near the church. As I continued, I began to wonder if I should not turnaround and go home. Things did not seem quite right. The pub was dark, the shop was dark, the estate of new houses was dark. There were no cars moving around. I could not see any signs of people except for the occasional flicker or flash of what Emmie calls a torch.

I reached the small row of cottages on the further outskirts of the village. There was another large tree branch down. It seemed to have previously been attached to a big tree which grew in front of the cottages, but it was now lying across the footpath over something. I thought it was a good thing the tree was still standing or at least one of the cottages might have been crushed. I suddenly heard a faint voice crying, "Help, help." I went closer to look, and there lay Colonel Snyppe under the fallen branch. I recalled he lived in one of the cottages.

"Oink, what are you doing there?" I queried politely.

"Don't hurt me, don't hurt me," he cried out, seeming surprisingly distressed.

"Of course I won't hurt you," I replied as politely as I could. "But you do seem to be in an odd place. Can I assist? Why are you down there?"

The colonel replied surprisingly courteously, "I foolishly went to check on my car during the storm, and I left my phone indoors. On the way back the tree came down on me and now I am stuck."

"It's a branch, not a tree, although it's quite big. Do you want me to see if I can move it?" I asked.

"Could you?" asked the colonel who appeared to be shivering and not his usual self. "My leg hurts and I am very cold."

I moved close to him and the tree branch. "You won't bite, will you?" he asked, showing a little of his normal attitude.

I showed my contempt with a grunt. Using my snout and strength from my upper body I pushed and pushed the offending branch. Eventually I shifted it, and the colonel was freed from being trapped by the wood but still seemed in great difficulty moving.

"I think I might have got a fracture to my leg," he said. "I don't think I can stand without help and I feel so cold."

"I could try to drag you to your house, oink," I said, "but I am concerned that could hurt you further. I think I should go and get some help... but before I go and get help is there anything I can do to help you get warm...? I mean I could blow on you I suppose."

"My house is not locked," said the colonel ignoring my offer. "It's number 3 with the red door just there." He pointed and continued, "Just inside the front door are some coat hooks with my spare coats and there is also a throw on the armchair near the door... please grab something... but don't do any damage." I grunted my contempt for the *suggestion that I could cause damage and headed to his cottage.*

The door easily opened when I gave a little push. I could not see very well because of the lack of light but I managed to pull down a big raincoat off a hook. I was concerned that the rest of the coats were too neatly arranged for me to remove them easily, and I was worried that I might get shouted at by the colonel for making a mess. In the gloom I could just about make out a chair with a rug on it which I took to be the throw he had requested. I pulled it off the chair easily. I could not see much else, and I thought I should return to the colonel quickly, so I retreated pulling the coat and the rug with my mouth. I got them as close to the colonel as I was able, so he was able to spread them over himself.

"Thank you," he said, still shivering.

I replied, "Now I am going to get some human help."

I reckoned I was nearest to either Rebecca or Derry and Terry and Sven. While I knew Rebecca would be kind, I also remembered Terry was an animal nurse. Maybe that was not so different to a human nurse. I decided to head for their house. I was not sure how they felt about the colonel, but I hoped they would help him.

It was just beginning to get light. The Mossesson house, Granary Manor, did not seem to have any lights on, but I heard several dogs barking loudly and there was some flickering from what I later found out were a mixture of torches and lanterns. I went down the track by the side of the house until I found the path to the front garden and front door. It had a metal door knocker on it in the shape of a cat's head with a big ring in its mouth. I managed with effort to stretch upward and get the ring in my teeth and knock loudly.

"Who on earth is that?" I just about heard Derry's voice from inside over the barking of the dogs.

"Shall I investigate?" said Sven.

"Be careful," said Derry. "It's a very odd hour to be banging on a door."

The door opened. There stood Sven with a lantern in one hand and a poker in the other hand.

"Patrick? What on earth are you doing there?" he asked. Derry and Terry peered around and there was a lot more barking in the background.

"There has been an accident... the colonel was hurt by a tree... oink..." I replied.

"Emmie will be angry you are out... we will need to get you home," said Sven. "What have you done to annoy the colonel now?"

"I haven't done anything wrong... but the colonel is hurt... a tree branch landed on him in the storm... come quickly... grunt," I responded.

Coats and boots were grabbed as was something called a 'First Aid Kit'. Sven carried a large torch, and they followed me down the lane to where the still colonel lay near his cottage.

"Thank you, thank you," said Colonel Snyppe from his position on the ground.

Sven immediately reached for his phone and rang for an ambulance.

"Because of the storm they say it may be some time," he said. I hoped they did not approach from Emmie's side of the village. I helped Sven move the tree branch further from the colonel and so it did not block up the lane and the ambulance could get close to the colonel. It was fairly heavy so we could only push and shove it.

Terry said to the colonel, "Do you mind if I strap up your leg...? I know I am a veterinary nurse not a human nurse... and we must do something to warm you up before hypothermia sets in badly..."

"You can see to my leg. Patrick the pig has already helped by *getting things to cover me or I would be a lot worse. In fact, I think I have been unfair to him…" the colonel said.*

"Don't bother with that just now," I said. "You need to be warmed up… I could cuddle up to you and breathe on you to warm you…" I offered again.

For some reason, the colonel looked uncertain. "That's very kind," he said. "I have some hot water bottles in my house and more rugs, which maybe someone can fetch? I expect you need to go home, pig."

Derry said she would go and get further rugs. She said that hot water bottles directly next to him could make things worse, but she would use things from indoors to gently warm him up. I did seriously wonder how things were at home with Emmie and Delores.

"Now you have some help… oink… I think I ought to go home. I hope you will be alright, Colonel," I said.

"Thank you for your help. I am sure someone can tell you how I get on," said the colonel sounding genuinely grateful. "I was unfair to you. I realise it now."

"I ought to go home before Emmie misses me," I said.

Derry, Terry and Sven promised to let me know how the colonel got on. I hurried to get back to the farm since it was becoming daylight. As I approached the turning to the farm, I noticed some men in yellow hard-hats with vans and a piece of equipment which could lift a man up. The vans said, 'Power East Gridlectric'. They seemed too busy mending wires and cables, so they did not notice me. I went up the farm track and crept back into my quarters pulling the door closed. I snuggled up to Delores and fell into a deep sleep.

Much later in mid-morning I awoke to hear the television working. Emmie was there with a bucket of food.

"We got the power back," she said. "It's been a terrible storm… you can't possibly have slept through it," she said to me. I was about

to confess to going out when the discussions about the storm conditions, storm damage and if it was caused by global warming were interrupted on the television by a big sign saying, 'Breaking News'. The television person said,

"Now we go live to Westminster for breaking news. Let's hear from our reporter Bradleigh Baggerton."

There was then television coverage of what I understood to be the Houses of Parliament with a cold looking man with a microphone standing outside.

"The Prime Minister Percy Vere has been under attack from his own party and the Opposition for failing to set up the Commission on Diversity and Equality on the British Island territories which has been seen as a precursor to the populations of the islands being empowered to address climate change and, in some cases, to having full independence. His own party has been very vocal after hurricanes blamed on climate change killed nearly a hundred people in these very islands. After months of inaction Home Secretary Clytemnestra Wylie-Boothe has said the Commission is now in being and will start work on Monday. The members and its chairperson will be announced tomorrow morning. Rumour has it that top judge and Honorary Law Professor His Honour Judge Winston Armstrong KC is first choice for the role. Can we expect him to jet off to the Pitcairn Islands next week?"

"Oh, no, oh no," I grunted. "We can't lose His Honour... That man Bilius will send people to get me."

Photos of both the Home Secretary and the judge flashed up on the screen. Bradleigh Baggerton described the career of His Honour Judge Armstrong KC.

"Many were expecting His Honour to be appointed to the High Court bench shortly. He is ideally suited for dealing with these issues *according to many who know him, but one wonders how he and the rest of the Commission will deal with the suddenness of their appointments. It is true many of these islands have issues of diversity and climate change which need addressing sooner rather than later, but there is speculation that Miss Wylie-Boothe has made this move to bolster her flagging career. Being appointed Home Secretary was always going to be a poisoned chalice and rumour has it the 'Welly Boot' as she is nicknamed made this sudden move to avoid being given the actual boot by the Prime Minister who has plenty of problems of his own with his party being divided over a number of issues."*

I was very upset and concerned and voiced my fears loudly to Emmie.

"Alright, alright," she said, looking concerned herself. "Stop all that grunting. I will try to ring His Honour late this afternoon when he rises from court. I agree this is a concern."

"There is something else," I added. "When the storm was stopping, I thought I ought to check the area... to make sure we were safe." It was a bit of what the humans called a fib. "I walked a little further than I intended and found the colonel on the ground hurt..."

"Patrick... you were told not to go out." Emmie looked cross. "And what did you do to the colonel... I hope you left him alone?"

Now I was cross. I made a loud contemptuous grunt. "I didn't do anything bad. I helped the colonel. He was hurt by a tree. I got help from Derry, Terry and Sven. Please could you telephone them and find out how he is?"

Emmie looked at me with a doubting look but made a call to Derry. I heard her say, "Yes," and "Hmm," a number of times, and finally, "I'll tell him."

"I am sorry I doubted you," said Emmie. "It seems without your

quick thinking things might have been a lot worse. Apparently, it took about two hours after you left for the ambulance to come. The paramedic said the colonel had probably got mild to moderate hypothermia from which he appeared to be recovering, but he had undoubtedly needed to have his leg treated. Terry went with him in the ambulance. She just phoned her mother. It appears the colonel has a broken leg. The hospital is looking for a bed for him on a Ward since they want to keep him in one or two nights. Because of the hypothermia as well as the leg... and his age. Derry is going to the hospital shortly to bring the colonel some things and pick up Terry." She paused. "The colonel sends a message to thank you very much. You may have saved his life."

"Oink," I said. "But who's going to save my life if that Bilius man goes after me?"

Delores who was not normally conversational looked worried and said to Emmie,

"Hey, no-one's gonna hurt my Patrick, are they?"

Emmie patted her,

"Not if I have anything to do with it," she said, sounding determined.

Chapter 11

It's never over, 'til it's over.

Patrick was the most upset I have ever seen him after he listened to the television bulletin which suggested His Honour might be sent overseas. Delores seemed to understand he was bothered, and therefore mirrored his upset. There were so many grunts and squeals, and they refused to eat their usual pig feed or anything else. Piecrust the dog could sense there was something wrong and began whining. Even the cats seemed to sense there was disquiet in the air. Their usually erect tails were flat, and they kept walking in circles outside Patrick's animal shed making mewing noises. When I fed the outdoor animals, I wondered if it was my imagination, but they seemed unduly subdued. Perhaps it was the effect of the storm.

Alain had managed to get out of the village once they had mended the power lines and was heading to court. I managed to speak to Mathilda in London on the phone, but being in an urban environment she was little affected by this particular storm, and not greatly interested in Patrick's fate. I rang Aaron at his university, and he confirmed that although there were some trees down on his campus, he was safe and well. He said with a laugh,

"Charlie was out dining with some posh boys dining club... he narrowly avoided getting a tree on his head. I am glad I kept indoors with my books even though it sounds a bit dull."

I was relieved he was distancing himself from some of Charlie's activities, although being knocked on the head by a tree might have improved Charlie's brainpower. I told Aaron about Patrick and the colonel, and the worry over Jonathan Bilius. He sent his best wishes to Patrick.

"Knowing you, Mum, you will sort it," he ended the conversation.

Rebecca had turned up and joined Letitia and I in the kitchen when I tried to ring His Honour. I could only get his Clerk who said,

"His Honour has sent you an email which he says should address the matter he knows you are pursuing."

I looked in my email box and saw an email had just arrived. It said,

'Dear Mrs Martyns,

I am aware you are concerned about the issue of Patrick White. Please tell him not to be worried. The matter will be addressed quite shortly. After you have both listened to the News tomorrow morning, we may be able to have a little chat,

Kind regards,'

It was a most curious email. I could not make out what to expect. I read it out to Rebecca, Letitia and also to Patrick. He seemed slightly reassured by it but still would not eat his pig food. All we could do was sleep on the matter.

Next morning, I was up really early after a restless night. I took my coffee into Patrick and sat with him as we watched the morning television shows. At eight o'clock a newsreader began to read the morning news. After about ten minutes the words, 'Breaking News' appeared on the screen.

"Let us go over to Bradleigh Baggerton at Westminster who has a Press release from the Home Secretary."

Bradleigh Baggerton was once again standing in Parliament Square looking chilly.

"Well, there has been considerable surprise this morning that the Chair of the Commission on Diversity and Equality on British Island Territories is not to be His Honour Judge Armstrong KC. The Chair of 'Codbit' as it is now known colloquially is the relatively unknown academic and barrister Assistant Professor Jonathan Bilius. A press release was made by the office of the Home Secretary just half an hour ago. If I can catch him, I am hoping to interview Professor Bilius this afternoon about his forthcoming tour of Pitcairn Islands, St. Helena, the Falkland Islands and other far flung British owned territories on the other side of the globe."

If a pig could be said to be laughing and smiling, then that is what Patrick was doing in between rolling around with his feet in the air! Piecrust started barking. There was a cacophony of noise. Letitia arrived to investigate.

"What is it? What is it?" she said. Patrick grunted and squealed a response.

"That dreadful man Bilius is off to the other side of the world!" he said.

At that moment, my phone began ringing. I hoped it was not some troublesome client or a salesman as the display said, 'private number'. It was His Honour Judge Armstrong KC.

"I trust you've seen the news?" he said. "I did tell you I would sort things out."

"However, did you fix it?" I asked.

"Well," said His Honour, "Clytemnestra used to be my pupil when I was at the Bar, and before she went into politics. While I was getting a lot of pressure to Chair 'Codbit' from some of her colleagues, the truth is I never wanted to do it. I have youngsters at home and my life is here and my ambitions are here. When you started to have a problem with Bilius it occurred to me that I could kill two birds with one stone. Bilius is super ambitious as you know, so I had a private word with Clytemnestra as to how good he would be leading 'Codbit'. Actually, it might be just his thing!"

"What about his family? I assume he is married because Alain mentioned daughters. How will any partner feel about this?" I queried.

"Probably glad to be rid of him for a while," said His Honour. "He has a charming wife, quite strangely given he is so irksome, but they do say opposites attract. She is an academic too, seemed very pleasant when I met her."

"Hopefully this ends Patrick's current problems," I said.

"Well, Bilius is having to take an eighteen-month sabbatical from the university. I can't see anyone else being upset that he became dung-covered playing football," said His Honour.

I thanked His Honour again and held the phone up so Patrick could thank him too.

"Well," said His Honour, "I owed it to you, because I was the one who got you over to the university in the first place. If I may I will visit you again in due course?"

Patrick grunted a "Yes."

The call ended.

"Now you can settle down to a quiet life," I said.

Patrick's life was still not going to be quiet.

Rebecca called in a few days later. It seemed that a group on the Parish Council led by Councillors Drydale and Oxtable were organising the annual village Christmas fete. It was to take place partly inside the village hall and partly outside it. She had been asked to make contact with Patrick and me. In past years, the colonel had dressed up as Santa and had sat in a grotto which someone had made for him. Although home from hospital and recovering, the colonel was unlikely to be well enough to fulfil his usual role. The Council group wondered if instead of having a grotto for Santa, I could not bring a trailer with Patrick inside. The children could then have a chance to say 'hello' to Patrick, and they hoped to cajole someone into playing an elf who would hand out a little gift to the children after they had seen Patrick.

On the face of it, the request for Patrick to take part in this village event, which occurred in early December did not seem as challenging as taking part in a mock trial, but I thought I should leave the decision to Patrick.

He grunted and sighed a little, "Always something, oink," he said. "Can't a fellow settle down?"

However, he agreed to play 'Santa pig' on condition that I stayed with him for the duration of the event and that the elf was played by someone who knew him. Rebecca and Letitia both volunteered for the role, which they agreed to share.

Patrick, it seemed, was in demand. The following day I received a telephone call from Colonel Snyppe. He seemed rather hesitant in his call. He cleared his throat,

"I do hope you don't mind me calling... it is really rather embarrassing. I just wondered if it would be possible for you to bring Patrick the pig to visit me. I can't go anywhere much at the moment since I'm on crutches. I wanted to thank him in person for saving my life and talk to him about... well... me being a bit fairer to animals."

I said I would have to ask Patrick.

"Oink," he said. "I suppose I could stroll down to him."

"I think I'd have to put you in the trailer." I sighed. "You can't go on your own."

Patrick grunted contemptuously. "Well, I've done it before..."

We hit on a compromise. I'd stick a bit of rope on him and I would walk with him. If anyone approached us, I would take hold of the rope and give the impression I was walking him. We would do our visit at dusk one day so hopefully we were less noticeable.

I rang the colonel and set the date and time, and soon one evening we walked together to the village.

"This is nice... oink..." said Patrick. I didn't comment.

I rang the doorbell at Colonel Snyppe's cottage. He opened the door, and I could see he was leaning on his crutches. There was a broad smile on his face,

"Would you like to come in?" he asked.

"I'm not sure that would be a good idea," I said noticing that the electric light shone on a china cabinet. Patrick just grunted. "Can I help you draw a chair up to the door so you can sit down and talk to Patrick?" I asked.

I helped the colonel draw up a chair to the open doorway and covered him in a throw as he made himself comfortable. He reached into a pocket as he finished settling himself. In his hand was a shiny green apple.

"May I give this to Patrick?" he asked. Although the strict rules might not have allowed this, I nodded my agreement.

Patrick grunted his thanks and took it gently from the colonel.

The colonel said, "I have never before met an animal like you, Patrick. You are truly remarkable. If you had not helped me, I might not be on the road to recovery."

Patrick grunted again. "Well, I didn't think you were supposed to be under that branch," he added.

The colonel said, "I have never apologised to a pig before for being prejudiced. And generally, I am not good at saying sorry. Is there anything I can do to make things up to you?"

Patrick replied with an "oink" and then said, "You could be nicer to Derry, Terry and Sven and their animals."

"Point taken," said the colonel. "I shall be thanking them properly too... and offering support to their animal rescue centre. I intend to make a New Year's resolution to take an interest in animal welfare."

We did not stay much longer. As we returned to the farm, Patrick asked,

"Could we walk to visit other people sometimes?"

I was non-committal, but I was pleased everything was settling down.

On the weekend of the Christmas fete, I looked in my mailbox and noticed an email I had missed. It said it was from the administrative assistant to the Dean of the Law faculty.

'Dear Mrs Martyns

I have been asked to contact you by the Dean following on from Mr Bilius' recent absence on sabbatical. The Dean has seen a copy of the letter from Mr Bilius to your good self. The Dean would like you to be aware that the letter was written to you without his knowledge or approval. So far as the Dean is concerned, he is aware that he agreed to an animal being brought to the university and he is sure you will not bring the said animal to the campus again unless of course you have prior written consent. There was a small amount of extra work needed by groundsmen to the soccer pitch. If you were to pay a token amount of £50 as a donation to the Dean's Charity (the bursary scheme for students in financial difficulty) all matters between the university and you relating to Patrick White, the pig will be closed. Please let me know if this is acceptable to you as soon as possible.

Regards Admin Assistant to the Dean of Faculty.'

The modest amount was one I was willing to pay. I decided to pay the amount and not tell Patrick about the email.

Patrick walked into the trailer quite happily that afternoon. I drove him the very short distance into the village. Rebecca and Letitia soon joined us dressed in elf outfits. We opened the top of the trailer. I decorated the opening with tinsel. I also managed to decorate Patrick in tinsel and balance a red Santa style hat on his head which I then secured with a bit of string. I had the ramp down so children could be taken up the ramp to visit Patrick under the close supervision of Letitia, Rebecca and myself. By the side of the trailer was a box containing chocolate selections for the children donated by Manny Sharma, and a large bucket of apples, turnips and swedes which I had brought from the farm for Patrick. Once the festival began, a local choir began to sing carols and other seasonal favourites.

Alain, Mathilda and Aaron were home for the weekend. Charlie was visiting as well. The four of them went into our village pub and came out with tankards of hot punch which were passed around.

"Can't I have one... oink...?" said Patrick.

"No," we all said as one. Having a drunk pig at the Christmas fete would not be a good idea.

There was an outside stall selling an eclectic mix of sausage rolls made by some village ladies, samosas made by Manny Sharma's family and mince pies made by Derry and Terry. Patrick looked on sadly as the humans tucked in but was placated with offerings from his bucket.

Mr Sharma was standing outside his shop smiling. He came over to us briefly.

"It is so good when the village comes together... Diwali, Chanukah, Christmas... it is all good," he said.

"Oink," said Patrick agreeing, looking hopeful. "I can smell there is a lot of food involved."

Rebecca hastened to give him a large apple as Mr Sharma

wandered off. Simon Christianson appeared.

"Hello, pig," he said in his usual Birmingham accent. "I'll try not to make pigs in blanket jokes about Christmas dinner."

He paused, "Did you know I might be co-opted onto the Council soon, so I can properly take part?"

Patrick grunted. "Anyway, have a great time," said Simon as he went on his way.

I could see the local bus pull in down the road and a number of passengers got off. I was able to make out Jake Daniels approaching, together with Anna who had played the usher at the mock trial. Jake had a large brown carrier bag with him. I was delighted they had decided to visit our festival.

"What's in the bag... oink...?" said Patrick sniffing the air.

Anna replied, "Sprouts and a cauliflower from my dad's allotment for Patrick."

"Thank you," said Patrick, and then rudely to Jake, "is this your girlfriend now?"

The young couple looked embarrassed but shyly held hands. Alain stepped in and offered to get them some punch from the pub. As everybody stood with glasses of punch in their hands, Jake smiled,

"Well, this is fun," he said. "And we have lost that awful Bilius for a time."

"Yes oink," said Patrick with a sort of piggy grin.

"Let's have a toast," said Jake raising his glass. "To a fantastic festive season and a great new year!"

At least Jonathan Bilius would be very busy for the next eighteen months, which after all was a long time in a pig's life.

Notes and Acknowledgements

First this is a work of fiction just like the first book about Patrick White, 'The World According to Patrick White', it does not pretend to give guidance or show any expertise on pig keeping. However, I must acknowledge being a regular reader of, 'Practical Pigs' magazine. I can also recommend, 'Raising Pigs' by Lee Faber published Abbeydale Press.

Further information on pig welfare can be found on www.britishpigs.org and of course with the RSPCA. 'The Country Smallholder' magazine published by Kelsey Media often has interesting information about pigs. Its predecessor, 'Country Smallholding' published by Archant had a particularly apt article written by Mandy Rickaby called, 'The pig paradox' in the November 2021 edition.

There is information on animal vocalisations on the website of the Zoological Society of London zslpublications.onlinelibrary.wiley.com/. More scientific minds than mine would have to explain, 'source filter theory' and the various abilities or otherwise of animals to speak.

Criminal procedure in the UK is governed by the Criminal Procedure Rules 2020.

https://www.gov.uk/guidance/rules-and-practice-directions-2020#criminal-procedure-rules-2020-contents

For more information about Courts in England and Wales see the website for HMCTS.

https://www.gov.uk/government/organisations/hm-courts-and-tribunals-service.

For information about the rules governing solicitors see the Solicitors' Regulation Authority website. https://www.sra.org.uk/

The Bar Council's website is https://www.barcouncil.org.uk/

Running a mock trial can be challenging. There is a good document by The Citizenship Foundation, 2003. info@citizenshipfoundation.org.uk. www.citizenshipfoundation.org.uk called 'Running a Mock Trial'. Precedents abound on the internet for criminal statements.

As for Parish Councils they are the lifeblood of many a village. Parish and Town Councils are the lowest tier of government in England. Parish and Town Councillors are unpaid volunteers, although the Clerk is usually a paid role, frequently part-time. Parish Councils as we know them, were established by the Local Government Act 1972. More information is available from https://www.nalc.gov.uk/.

I would make it plain that the antics of Cobblemarkham Parish Council are very much from the world of fiction. This book is intended to entertain so that the fictional parish council just like the fictional judge, lawyers and academics and other characters are to be viewed in that context; after all what real Parish Council would allow a pig to be involved with it?

Information about Suzanne Stephenson and her books

I would like to thank you for taking the time to read my books. If you have a moment to spare to review the book you have been reading, I would appreciate it. You may have your own thoughts about what I have written and that is fine. I was a lawyer for many years and then a District Judge. Any legal background is inspired by my long legal career although I hasten to stress the fictional nature of the humans. I am also privileged to live in the English countryside, surrounded by animals who provide a lot of inspiration, as did the bear I saw on holiday in Canada who sparked off the ideas for "Bearswood End". I enjoy sketching and the animal pictures are often sketches of animals around the farm. I sometimes think the animals are in charge.

I want to give particular thanks to Sarah Luddington from Mirador Publishing who took me and the animal inspired books under her wing.

If you want to contact me, please feel free to look at my Instagram: Suzanne Stephenson (@bearswood_end).

Or contact me through the website:

https://stephensons-authors.co.uk/

Email address: adventures@stephensons-authors.co.uk

The following are books I have written:

Bearswood End

A scientist wanders out into the wilderness and finds a mysterious village populated by bears. To be accurate the bears find him. Can the secret village of the bears survive a threat from the outside world? Read the scientist's diary and the story of the woman who finds it.

Mr Perkins takes Charge

A black cat walks into a solicitors' office. Lives change of the lawyers and people who cross this cat's path, usually for the better. Is he just a stray cat and is it all a co-incidence or is there something more mysterious afoot? If you like cats, you may find this intriguing. If you are just curious about the goings-on of a lawyers' office satisfy your curiosity following the trail of sunshine left by Mr Perkins' paws.

Waste

This is a legal satire about activities at a combined court in a fictional Northern town. Two young people arrive whose lives might otherwise have gone to waste and make fresh starts in this fictional town which boasts as main industries a waste plant and a sausage factory. Meet the Judges, MPs and other local characters.

Forever Waste

A more in depth look at the goings in within Waste encompassing a Romcom and sequels to the original book. You will find romance against the background of the court, its lawyers and judges and this Northern City and its politicians, and there is even an election in the city. You will also understand the highs and lows of the local football club, and you may even decide to copy a few recipes.

The World According to Patrick White

This is a comic tale with a pinch of satire about a lawyer who finds she has a talking pig, and we discover how he sees the human world and what he thinks of some of our habits and human foibles. Find out how the lawyer and her family cope with this pig of a situation. Needless to say, pig and human have a few adventures before the tale is over, including a court case where the pig is an expert witness and an encounter with a Royal dignitary.

A Cat's Judgement, Mr Perkins lays down the law

That mysterious black cat shows up at a bed and breakfast and a courthouse and things begin to change. Whether it is pet rescue, support animals or British sign language make your mind up if this is a stray moggy or is there a little bit of stardust on his paws.

The Tale of Philida Thrush,
A Children's poem about nature, home and community

When a song thrush has her nest demolished by the builders what can a bird do but look around town for a new home? Assisted by her friends Philida goes on a quest to find somewhere to live.

Printed in Great Britain
by Amazon